SHERLOCK
THE CASE
OF
THE EMPTY TOMB

SHERLOCK:
THE CASE
OF
THE EMPTY TOMB

PER EWERT

Foreword by Gary Habermas

WIPF & STOCK · Eugene, Oregon

SHERLOCK: THE CASE OF THE EMPTY TOMB

Wipf & Stock
An Imprint of Wipf and Stock Publishers
199 W. 8th Ave., Suite 3
Eugene, OR 97401

www.wipfandstock.com

PAPERBACK ISBN: 978-1-5326-6514-1
HARDCOVER ISBN: 978-1-5326-6515-8
EBOOK ISBN: 978-1-5326-6516-5

Manufactured in the U.S.A.   12/20/18

All Bible quotes from New English Translation, unless otherwise noted.

"For this reason I was born, and for this reason I came into the world - to testify to the truth. Everyone who belongs to the truth listens to my voice."

CONTENTS

FOREWORD by Gary Habermas • ix
PREFACE • xiii

Chapter 1
221B • 1

Chapter 2
THE GAME IS ON • 6

Chapter 3
A HIGH-LEVEL MEETING • 11

Chapter 4
LOOKING DEATH IN THE EYE • 16

Chapter 5
DEATH ON A CROSS • 22

Chapter 6
A KNOWN GRAVE • 29

Chapter 7
THE SCIENCE OF DEDUCTION • 37

Chapter 8
A FRAGMENT OF TRUTH • 45

Chapter 9
SUNDAY EXCURSION • 52

Chapter 10
TOMB DESERTED • 56

Chapter 11
ON THE ROAD • 63

Chapter 12
A CASE OF CORRUPTION • 70

Chapter 13
THE KEY IN A LETTER • 77

Chapter 14
SEARCHING FOR GRAVE ROBBERS • 84

Chapter 15
WHO DEVISES PLANS? • 90

Chapter 16
CROSS-EXAMINATION • 98

Chapter 17
THE CRUX OF THE MATTER • 107

Chapter 18
TURNING POINT • 113

Chapter 19
A NEW DOOR OPENS • 119

Chapter 20
THROUGH THE HAZE • 125

Chapter 21
DIVIDED THEY FALL • 131

Chapter 22
VISIONS AND REVELATIONS • 136

Chapter 23
ALL SAID AND DONE • 143

Chapter 24
DAWN BREAKS • 147

FOREWORD

THIS ADVENTURE CONCERNS THE great Sherlock Holmes and his well-known sidekick, physician John Watson! The renowned Holmes has been called "the most famous" character in English fiction and perhaps the most widely known fictional figure in the world." Further, "Holmes calls to mind one of the most widely known of all writers, Arthur Conan Doyle, who created Sherlock Holmes."[1]

Dr. Watson, on the other hand, may remind readers of Doyle's own past. The fictional character Sherlock Holmes was originally based on a historical person, Dr. Joseph Bell, who was one of Doyle's medical school professors at Edinburgh University.[2]

What a provocative setting as well as a creative means of beginning a volume of this nature! What would the famous fictional detective Sherlock Holmes have to do with perhaps the most famous event in human history—the resurrection of Jesus Christ? It is here that we begin our own journey in this volume, as the intriguing crossover matchup of this brilliant detective who was sure to be up to the task of untangling the very toughest and most exasperating of legal cases with the potential event which, if it actually occurred, would be the *sine qua non* of history.[3]

---

1. Sir Arthur Conan Doyle, *Conan Doyle Stories: Six Notable Adventures of Sherlock Holmes* (New York: Platt and Munk, 1960), "About Arthur Conan Doyle," 493.

2. Ibid., 494.

3. For history buffs, some of these elements may be reminiscent of the book, "The Trial of the Witnesses of the Resurrection of Jesus" (1729), written by Thomas Sherlock and going through many print editions in England and Europe.

THE RESURRECTION OF JESUS

Enough about Sherlock Holmes for now, as his exploits here are recast in this exciting novel. The author, Per Ewert, is a history teacher and scholar who remains both an admirer of the past as well as a student of good fiction. This combination prepares us and gets us started for this creative journey.

Perhaps to the surprise of many, the resurrection of Jesus is not some religious tale of long ago that fails to interest the intellectually stout-of-heart today. Surprisingly to some, even numerous skeptical scholars who specialize in New Testament subjects often study and interact regularly with this topic. In fact, the historical nature of Jesus' resurrection can be argued based on just a handful of historical facts surrounding this occurrence that are acknowledged by virtually all critical scholars who research these subjects. As such, quaint faith responses, religious jargon, or believing the inspiration of the New Testament are unnecessary prerequisites, making it an apt subject for historical dialogue.[4]

ENTER SHERLOCK HOLMES AND DR. WATSON

This Twenty-First Century team of Sherlock Holmes and his assistant, Dr. Watson, as portrayed in Ewert's novel, sorts out and checks in step by step fashion the medical, historical, and other potential data on behalf of the death and resurrection appearances of Jesus. How could such a case possibly be tested and argued? Sherlock and Watson plow their way through multiple experimental and research formats, gathering hints from morgues and medical experiments alike. A few experts are consulted and mysteries are solved.

For example, what were the most prominent and relevant customs in First Century Israel? Are there hints in the Gospels that truthful reports are even being presented? What do we know about crucifixion and why do the victims usually die? What could have happened to Jesus' dead and buried body? How is it even possible in this day and age to believe that Jesus was raised and appeared to his followers? Perhaps some alternative though quite natural solutions will better solve this entire matter?

Holmes and Watson pursue many avenues and settings as any modern detectives might, not at all in a religious or believing fashion. In the process,

---

4. For details, see Gary R. Habermas and Michael R. Licona, *The Case for the Resurrection of Jesus* (Grand Rapids, MI: Kregel, 2004).

some surprising events occur, including the discovery of both dead ends and solid leads alike. Incredibly, Watson unexpectedly finds that Sherlock has simulated his own crucifixion with the famous detective himself as the victim! But through it all, the work proceeds to its end, including a bit of a surprise ending.

Some readers will no doubt be surprised to find that this investigative duo refuse to settle for the regular venue of answers, either. For example, even if the known events were to point more favorably in the direction of Jesus having appeared to his followers after his death, how could anyone dare to believe that such nonsense is even possible? After all, executed men do not rise from the dead and we do not stumble across resurrections in our everyday world! Warning: Sherlock Holmes' creative way of approaching this particular issue is not one that will be discovered in any apologetics text!

But Sherlock and Watson do get to invoke their well-known maxim that when possible options—unthinkable and impossible though they may be—have been eliminated, leaving only one solution, the remaining option is the truth.[5] This rule comes into play here, too, in a fascinating way.

Throughout, this story is a fresh and exciting read. It is definitely not just some often-heard, dusty tale adapted from an ancient Sunday School lesson. A few brief textual notes even direct interested readers to sources for the pursuit of additional research matters. From start to finish, it is a new approach to a perennial topic that holds one's interest as leads are tracked down while different paths and angles are pursued.

These trails may conceivably be similar to the ones that the original Sherlock Holmes may well have taken himself if he had been the one searching for the best answers here. Time and again, the crafty techniques invoke a smile, accompanied by thoughts of, "how could he tell that?" which occur just prior to the reason being given. In this sense, it is not a religious book per se, tone written for believers alone. It deserves to be read, enjoyed, and recommended widely.

Gary Habermas
Distinguished Professor and Chair of the Dept. of Philosophy and Theology, Liberty University

5. As seen in Doyle's collected stories above, "The Sign of the Four," page 234, and in the conclusion here.

PREFACE

Since I was a teenager, I have nurtured a strong fascination for two very different people—one real and one fictitious—the wandering Jewish rabbi and healer Jesus of Nazareth, and the strictly analytical detective Sherlock Holmes. I have studied and admired the stories that have been written about their thoughts and deeds. Both of them have had an appeal that has spanned through different times and cultures, and still today in the third millennium, they awaken huge interest across the world.

In the adventure you are about to read, I have transposed the well-known characters Sherlock Holmes and his flatmate and co-worker John H. Watson to a contemporary setting. Still, I have taken care to preserve the personalities and the atmosphere from the original stories by Conan Doyle. At the same time, I have tried to figure out how a person like Sherlock Holmes would have addressed the remarkable circumstances which took place during that Passover some two thousand years ago—events which have had such a dramatic effect on the history of the world ever since. The task before me has been to give a picture of what might have happened if the world's greatest detective would have taken on the most renowned disappearance in history—The Case of the Empty Tomb.

Readers who mainly wish to follow the story from beginning to end can do so without letting yourself be interrupted. However, for those who wish to dig deeper into the historical evidence for the factual information presented by the characters in the book, I have added this in footnotes. This book may hereby be read at two levels: either as an exciting adventure about two peculiar cases begging a solution, or as a more academic account about the historical support for the resurrection of Jesus.

I hope that you who already are accustomed to the characters in the book will feel familiar with how they are portrayed. My hope is also that this book would awaken an interest among those who have still not begun a closer relation to the detective at Baker Street, or the preacher from Nazareth. It could be the case that this story might inspire a closer acquaintance with both.

There are some people to whom I am extra grateful for their input during this project. Some years ago, I got to know Gary Habermas and function as his interpreter on a speaking tour in Sweden. On a personal level, this was also a quite difficult period in my life. I am deeply thankful for Gary's friendship and advice, and for contributing with a foreword to this English edition. My gratitude also to Grace Olaison, who has been of invaluable use for advice on British culture and the fine nuances in the English language.

I now wish you welcome home to the familiar domains of Sherlock Holmes. Let the game begin!

Forserum, Sweden, a dark January night 2019,
Per Ewert

CHAPTER I

221B

AT FIRST, SHE HESITATED for a second, but then Mrs Hudson lifted her hand and knocked gently at the door. Nobody opened. She waited for another moment. Not a sound could be heard from inside. As the door appeared to be unlocked, she gently turned the doorknob and put the letters on the stool next to the door.

It's really incomprehensible how two grown men can avoid taking care of such a basic thing as collecting their own mail, she reflected, and thought back on the days when first one and then the other of the two bachelors moved into the lodgings on the second floor at 221B Baker Street. It should just be temporary, they had said. But now both of them started to feel like permanent fixtures in the building. Yes, life had definitely changed since their arrival, the old landlady thought to herself. Experience had taught her that she ran the risk of meeting virtually anyone, or any*thing* behind this door—which was also the reason for her caution when entering.

She quickly surveyed the flat and found that the living-room had the curtains closed. The kitchen, however, had light coming in from outside, she noticed. What the two small bedrooms looked like nowadays she dared not even think about. Especially the tall one's. He appeared to her as quite unpredictable, and at times he left a ghastly mess around him. What sort of profession he actually had, she still couldn't really put her finger on. He seemed not to have an office to go to, as far as she could understand. Nevertheless, he appeared to perform some kind of tasks for the radically different types of people who occasionally visited the flat upstairs.

But how he worked, when he really got going with whatever-it-was-he-did! Day or night, weekday or weekend, nothing seemed to matter when he actually put himself to work. Maybe there was some sort of psychiatric instability deep down, she thought sometimes. He didn't want to be disturbed under any circumstances, and he could be terribly touchy when he had his most active periods. There was definitely something that separated him from normal people. A tendency towards bipolarity, perhaps? Mrs Hudson had never dared to ask about the state of her tenant's mental health. God knows how he would have reacted?

Things were very different with the other man in the lodgings, she thought. At least he had a proper job. Well, or at least a proper title. Doctor. Or, to be more specific: army doctor. He didn't mention his background much, but it was clear that he'd had some difficult experiences during his missions in Afghanistan. Either way, things seemed to be in order with him. He kept his personal belongings considerably tidier, and he had more normal habits. One could probably hope that he would be on his way back to a normal job as a doctor after being medically discharged from the army, as he appeared to have been.

The old lady carefully backed out through the entrance again, in order to return down to her own premises.

"Mrs Hudson!" The words came sharply from the duskier areas further back in the living-room. She jerked at the unexpected sound.

"Oh, excuse me, Mr Holmes. It was certainly not my intention to disrupt. You were working?" she wondered, without actually knowing exactly where to look.

"Definitely not. *Definitely* not . . . " sighed a voice from the swivel chair by the darkened window. The man in the chair swung around, threw a quick glance at his landlady and continued with poorly concealed irritation. "Working is most certainly the thing I'm *not* doing at present."

Mrs Hudson looked at her watch. A dressing gown on a grown man at two o'clock in the afternoon wasn't exactly an indication of maturity and responsibility, she thought to herself.

"I took the liberty of bringing your mail up here, Mr Holmes." She gave an almost invisible bow.

"What's in it? Please, say it's something that could give at least a scrap of dynamic to life!"

The landlady quickly eyed through the three envelopes that had arrived. "Well, if you don't intend to take the trouble of getting up and seeing for yourself, I would guess . . . bills. But they are as usual addressed to Mr Watson."

Suddenly, footsteps were heard from the stairs. Mrs. Hudson recognized them. Surely, they had become more resolute compared to when he first moved in. Yes, he would indeed soon be strong enough to find both a job and start a family, she thought.

"Good afternoon, Mrs Hudson," he said politely while passing her. "Good . . . morning, Sherlock," he continued in a more tired tone of voice when he discovered the restless figure in the chair. He lifted up the shopping bags on the kitchen table.

"Could you check the mail, John?" came the voice from the chair. "For God's sake, may it be a letter bomb or some other refreshing material, *something* that can give my life a tiny little bit of challenge!"

John H. Watson weighed the small pile of letters in his hand. "Seems to me like extremely common mail, I fear."

Sherlock Holmes threw his arms up in despair. He let them fall down by the sides of the chair and exclaimed: "I can't take it any longer!"

"You haven't seen any signs that he's started to take any strange substances?" whispered Mrs Hudson in John's ear. He shook his head, and she continued, now louder: "Had a fruitful day in town, Dr Watson?"

"Oh yes, I've managed to get a few small errands done. Nothing major. Saw something a bit odd, by the way!" He gave a short laugh. "Down by Paddington Green I ran into a guy with a black cross on his forehead. You know I've been trying to study your methods, Sherlock, and I just started to think whether it might be some kind of group identification. But as I looked up towards the Church of Saint Mary, I noticed a number of people coming with similar crosses on their foreheads. It may have been some kind of . . . "

"Ash Wednesday," the voice from the chair interrupted. Sherlock had once again turned his face away towards the window.

"So this is a familiar tradition to you?" John asked, slightly surprised.

"I can't say that I've studied the spiritual meaning of the day, but I'm familiar with the crosses on the foreheads," Sherlock answered, and came strolling out towards the kitchen. "Some years ago I almost made the same mistake you made initially. I therefore saw the need to pursue a deep study of signs and symbols that people wear, as well as the circumstances with which they're connected. It's actually been quite an important tool in order to place people in the correct context."

"But you don't know the religious meaning of the day itself?"

"Not really." Sherlock started looking through what was in the new shopping bags.

"Without being a terribly dedicated church-goer I can tell you that Ash Wednesday marks the beginning of Lent," Mrs Hudson noted. "With Lent obviously being the 40-day-long period before Easter," she added.

"Surely so, but still of little practical importance," Sherlock murmured, while seeming very focused upon the goods from the supermarket. Abruptly he cried: "Quinoa! Is that really food for a grown man?"

Mrs Hudson, having no intention to act as a nutritionist for the two gentlemen, took her leave and quietly slipped from the flat.

"And surely you know the meaning of the Easter holiday?" wondered John carefully, without being certain if he actually wanted to hear the reply.

"That information I have gladly handed over to theologians and anthropologists," Sherlock smiled, although not very heartily.

"Not a clue?" John responded grimly.

"At least not enough to give a full account."

John sighed, and started to put the shopping away. Sherlock leaned back against the kitchen worktop and looked on. Suddenly he twitched, as if hit by an insight:

"Didn't you buy any mustard? You know, we've been out of mustard for at least a week."

His roommate shut a cupboard door with a bang.

"Sherlock, you can't be serious! Easter is one of the main festivals in British culture!"

"Yes, yes, I know the story. Jesus, the cross, and so on. But as a consulting detective it's of far greater importance to me to be able to trace the different kinds of poison that could be hidden in an Easter meal, than to know the exact background of the holidays when these meals are eaten."

"Sherlock Holmes—I have to say that you probably have the most unevenly distributed body of knowledge I've met in any human being!"

"Precisely!" exclaimed Sherlock. By the tone of his voice he seemed quite content by this judgement. "My view is that the brain is like a vault. When it's full—it's full. On that basis it would be quite inappropriate to fill it up with garbage that you don't need for your work. It steals time, it steals focus, it steals capacity that could be better used for other material."

"Present-day neural scientists probably wouldn't agree with that description," John objected in a careful effort to stress his own medical competence.

"Since when have neural scientists achieved anything of practical importance?" sniffed Sherlock. "No, my simple experience tells me that subjects like philosophy, religion and the like are of quite little value in crime investigations."

"My dear friend!" replied John in an indignant tone. "You're a thinking—most people would even say extremely intelligent person. Don't you ever ponder over the great questions about life, universe and everything?"

"Absolutely. But each time I end up with the conclusion that these questions must be delegated to more mystically oriented people. We don't have enough evidence to give satisfactory answers. I'm dedicated to facts, not to mythological speculation."

Sherlock retreated back to his seat, tumbled down in it, and hid his head in his hands. Soon enough he flew back up again, staring frantically:

"But what should a man do when he so seldom meets a real challenge? Are my abilities supposed to just moulder away, unused, wasted on nothing?" Sherlock exhaled a long sigh. "Lost necklaces, unfaithful husbands, inquiries about the perfect Lotto system . . . " Deeply frustrated, he banged his fist against the armrest. "Where are the really stimulating mysteries just waiting to be solved?"

John came along into the living-room, and took a seat in the sofa to open the mail. He stretched for the penknife and said, more or less to himself:

"The first Easter, eh? That would have been something for a sharp-eyed Roman investigator." He barked a short laugh: "One executed prisoner, mission accomplished and . . . boom—all of a sudden they stand there with an empty tomb! Well, isn't that something . . . "

The conversation came to an end. The only thing that broke the silence was the sound of the ripping of envelopes and flicking through of papers. Had John H Watson lifted his eyes, he would have seen that something had changed in the other man's appearance. The listless expression on his face had disappeared, and was now replaced by intense concentration.

Sherlock sprang up from his chair, his eyes crystal clear, in that unmistakable way that bore witness that something had awoken inside his brain. He turned to John and emphatically declared: "I'll take the case!"

CHAPTER 2

THE GAME IS ON

JOHN LOOKED UP IN surprise. It took a few moments before he understood what Sherlock meant. Still, he felt that he had to double-check the matter.

"You'll take the . . . case?"

"The empty tomb. Peculiar case. Those inspire me. Let's see, how do we begin?"

Sherlock started wandering around in the room, curiously waiting for a response from his companion. John sighed: "Don't be ridiculous. The events in question took place two thousand years ago, in case you've missed that."

"Since when have I let a time lapse stop me from taking up an interesting case?"

"But..?" The good doctor felt that he ran out of words.

"Come on, John!" Sherlock sat himself down on the armrest of the armchair on the opposite side of the coffee-table, and enthusiastically leaned forward towards his flatmate. "There are no impossible cases. Some just take a little more time. So what have we here?" Sherlock flung his arms wide. "We have one empty tomb and one missing body. What we need to do is gather all available facts, sort out possible scenarios, and then methodically and without mercy test these until the correct one remains." Sherlock took a pause to breathe. "Besides, I don't have anyone chasing me with their problems right now. Well, nobody but that woman Hensworth and her missing pedigree cat."

"Have you solved that?"

"Dear me!" Sherlock stared in frustration. "She's forgotten it at her neighbour's, thrown it in the garbage, eaten it or whatever. If I am to keep my brain cells fully functional, I need to find something challenging. Preferably something with difficult and quite unexpected elements. Those things make an investigation more complicated—but still far from impossible."

"Absolutely. Very thrilling indeed," John replied in an unsympathetic tone. "Please go ahead and lose yourself into antique mysteries as much as you like. Myself, I have more down-to-earth business to take care of."

John adjusted his jacket and opened his laptop, while Sherlock without further ado disappeared into his room. John Watson had experienced a lot together with this intellectually brilliant but utterly unpredictable partner. Therefore, he rarely became surprised by Sherlock's whims and outbursts. Admittedly, he did have some good points too, only they were all too often concealed behind this impatient and immature behaviour that sometimes made Sherlock Holmes look like a spoiled overgrown schoolboy, rather than a brilliant professional in his prime time in life.

John shook his head and opened the web browser, in order to take care of today's errands. A moment later Sherlock returned, newly shaven and well-dressed, and interrupted John's train of thoughts.

"Well then, let's get started!" The petulant expression from five minutes ago was now completely gone from Sherlock's face, replaced by a strong zeal in his eyes. "I would need access to all available facts concerning this case. Do you have a good idea of what mode of procedure to take from now?"

John snapped back: "You can't be serious, Sherlock! Here I sit, trying to find a decent used car, and then you come up with . . . " John leaned back in the sofa, looked up into the ceiling and tried to decide whether he should try to open up a serious conversation or not. He closed his eyes, swallowed and continued: "What in the name of heaven do you actually mean?"

"John, you have been of invaluable help to me several times before." Sherlock cautiously sat down opposite his friend, his voice sounding honourably kind. "If it wasn't for your faithful assistance, many cases would have been buried. And most probably myself too, for that matter."

Sherlock turned his eyes towards the floor. An observant viewer would have noted the slight blush on his cheeks. John sighed. He knew that when his detective friend finally had got started on a particular route, there was nothing in the entire Commonwealth that could pull him back again.

"Sometimes I don't understand your reasoning," John continued in a tired voice. "But this time I don't even understand your point of departure.

You can't take a "case" that's two thousand years old. There are no witnesses left, and all possible physical remains are since long gone."

John paused to think. "Yes, religion may certainly have a value for people, maybe even in some way for me personally. But this is nothing that you can, or should try to investigate as a detective."

"I would say the opposite," replied Sherlock. "There is perhaps no area where deduction is as important as when it comes to religion. Now, if there are statements within the religious realm that are testable, just like all other factual propositions, then it's also possible to take a scientific approach towards them."

Sherlock took a break, and thought the thing over once more: "I don't deny that there may be some kind of spiritual benefit in faith, although this may not be one of my strongest character traits. Therefore it's so valuable to have a trusted friend like you, John!" smiled Sherlock and patted his flatmate's arm encouragingly. "I suspect that you're at least a bit sharper than me on the spiritual field!"

John shook his head. "I wouldn't bet on that. I guess I'm like most other modern Brits. Questions about God and faith I usually keep quite private." John now felt compelled to return to the main question.

"But let's talk straight now: you're some kind of consulting detective of the twenty-first century. If you right out of the blue want to change careers and become a religious historian, I certainly won't be the one to object. Though I haven't seen any such tendencies up until ten minutes ago. Am I right?"

"Yes, yes . . . " Sherlock's head came down, and he shook it slowly. "But do you have even the slightest idea of what it means for me to be out of active cases, John? I become like . . . a shrivelled raisin, like a cat shut inside a sack! I become crazy, do you understand me?" Sherlock grabbed his friend's collar with both hands and stared him in the eye. "I've got to get out of that sack! I've got to get a problem to wrestle with—otherwise I'll die!"

"Then go out and buy a book of Sudoku or something!" John roared back and rid himself of Sherlock's hands.

This time, things had gone too far for the otherwise so calm doctor. Months of treading carefully in order not to upset his flatmate's peace of mind now took its toll. He continued angrily: "I can't deal with these outbursts of yours, as if you were the only person in the world to get a bit fed up with life sometimes! Maybe it's time that you start taking care of shopping, bills and other stuff like normal people! Why not accept that every day can't go at maximum speed—not even for Sherlock Holmes!"

John interrupted himself. Had he lost his head now? Had he overdone it? Sherlock fell back in his chair, closed his eyes, waited a few seconds and replied:

"I know . . . I know . . . Forgive me, John. You're the only one I can be really straightforward with. But this is the way I feel. It's no good for me to walk around idle. And . . . " Sherlock nodded in John's direction. "Apparently it isn't very good for other people around me either."

John remained silent, then came to grips with himself again, stroked his hand over his unshaven chin and said: "No, no. It was me that was carried away. But you . . . you need to find a way to handle *both* those days when a lot happens, and those days when nothing at all seems to happen."

"Well then, John—let's try to review the situation." Sherlock regained his controlled calmness. "No inspector from Scotland Yard has called for assistance here today. No clients or debt collection agencies have knocked on the door. We can do whatever we want!" Sherlock hopefully clapped his hands and continued:

"Alright then! Let's now—purely hypothetically—imagine that we would want to examine a two thousand year-old death, where the corpse seems to have disappeared without a trace, and where we can't conduct a decent crime scene examination or witness interviews. Still, this is a disappearance that without hesitation has had a huge impact on the world since then. Doesn't that sound like something that could cheer up a depressed detective? Now, what did Mrs Hudson say, how much time is it between today and Easter?"

"Forty days, if my memory doesn't fail me completely . . . "

"OK, here's the deal. I'll take this case. If I haven't been able to solve it before Easter, I won't mention the thing ever again. And if some urgent present-day business shows up I'll drop this. Deal?"

John looked rather tired, and answered slowly: "I haven't stood in your way in any other case you've taken on. I won't do it this time either. Though I'm not sure that I could be of very much help here."

Sherlock seemed to pretend that he hadn't heard the last few words, and continued eagerly:

"With your assistance then, I would like to get access to as much factual information as possible about the events in question, so that we thereafter may form a well-founded opinion about what actually happened.

Do you wish to use the Internet or the library? You may choose first!" smiled Sherlock in an attempt of Abrahamic benevolence.

"I think it might be wise for you to take a trip out in town. A little air could do you good. I'd be glad to sit back here for a while. I need to visit a few used car sites as well, you know." John moved his fingers quickly in the air, as if writing on an invisible keyboard.

"So be it," replied Sherlock. He rose from the armchair and took the few steps towards the door. Before he crossed the threshold he stopped, turned his head back and said in a restrained voice: "John—the game is on. The first question we need to answer is: Can we with certainty establish that we have a dead body?"

The door slammed, and the footsteps vanished down the stairs. In the company of this man, no day is like another, thought John and returned to the computer screen. Two minutes later all reflections on ancient mysteries were gone, and his thoughts completely focused on petrol consumption and mileage.

CHAPTER 3

A HIGH-LEVEL MEETING

THE CALENDAR HAD PASSED mid-March. The sun shone from a clear-blue sky, and the first signs of spring started to show up in the parks and green areas in London. Chaffinches were heard singing in the trees, and daffodils were coming up in the flower beds.

John Watson took the stairs up from the underground at Victoria Station. A ping came out of his pocket. He took out his phone and read the incoming text.

<Where r u?>

Sherlock had a rather concise way of texting, today was no exception. They hadn't really spent a lot of time together the last fortnight or so. Exactly where Sherlock had spent his days, John didn't know for sure. He had kept to his standard strategy of not asking Sherlock directly what he was up to. Sooner or later he usually got dragged in anyway, if he liked it or not. John wrote a quick response:

<Victoria. Seeing colleague fr Afghanistan>

John kept his phone in his hand. Sherlock had two replying habits: either immediately or not at all, but very seldom anything between. This time the answer came within seconds.

<Suitable mortuary behind cathedral. Be there 1800>

John sighed. Things were apparently back on again. It was probably a new case that had kept Sherlock occupied for the last days. John had experienced a few morgue visits like this earlier. In the beginning he had felt acknowledged, convinced that Sherlock had use of his medical competence. It soon became clear, though, that Sherlock's own knowledge about dead bodies and causes of death were considerably larger than his, at least when it came to more peculiar cases. Over time they had seen more wounded human corpses together than most people would consider suitable.

John looked at his watch. Half past two. That would give him at least three hours until he was to enter the familiar atmosphere of cold-storage room and an examination of yet another victim of accident, or possibly worse. He ought to spend the time until then well. With firm steps he went into the pub for his afternoon date.

†

On time, John appeared at the announced place. The building appeared to be some kind of nursing home. Nothing but a small sign by the side door indicated that the lower floor also contained a morgue. By the entrance waited a young woman in green scrubs. She kept tapping nervously with her left foot, John noted.

"I was to meet Sher . . . " The woman didn't let him finish, but beckoned eagerly with her finger to make him come in.

She opened the door, and quickly led her visitor down a staircase, dimly lit by wall-mounted fluorescent strips on the wall. John discerned this was no situation for inane small-talk. Down in the basement they turned right through a corridor, ending by a heavy metal door, which the woman quickly opened and went through, immediately followed by her visitor.

"John, quick!" came a half-choked but familiar voice from above.

John twitched, turned half around, and looked upwards in astonishment. Hanging with his hands firmly gripped around a metal bar almost three yards above the floor was Sherlock Holmes.

John got that peculiar feeling where you suddenly find yourself in a completely unforeseen situation, realize that you ought to do something immediately, but can't make the brain tell the muscles exactly what to do. He didn't stand paralyzed for more than two seconds, but it made Sherlock gasp out once more: "For God's sake, John! Blood pressure, pulse and blood sample—now!"

Without a word, the woman handed over the suitable medical instruments to John, still so confused that he couldn't come up with a word to say. Sherlock still hung on the bar with his hands about a yard apart, carrying almost whole his body weight. His toes just barely touched a box underneath. John glanced up at his partner and saw that his wrists were attached to the bar with leather straps. Sherlock let his head fall down, closed his eyes and made a wry face. John's professional experience took over. He jumped up on the box beside his friend and went to action. Sherlock's arms and upper body were shaking a bit, but the pulse was still easy to find. With the hanging detective panting beside his head, John managed to perform the three ordered tests in about a minute.

"Done!" he proclaimed and triumphantly lifted the blood pressure equipment in the air as if it were a war-trophy.

"Cut me down!" said Sherlock in a feeble voice. The woman took out a scalpel and cut at the straps, while John held his friend in his arms to relieve the weight until the wrists were loosened. Then Sherlock slid down in a wordless and powerless heap on the concrete floor.

There he lay, alternately panting and coughing for some time, while neither John nor the young woman said anything. When his breathing had calmed down a bit, Sherlock lifted his head, looked straight at John and said weakly, though with emphasis: "Eighteen-o-two!"

Once more, it took John Watson a few seconds before he could understand the context. Sherlock continued: "You came . . . " He had to take a break to cough. "You came two minutes past. Not six o' clock! Do you possibly have any idea what it's like to hang at length on a bar like this?"

"Not really," John answered dryly. "Though, would you be so kind as to explain this bizarre experiment in sports medicine to me?"

Sherlock took a few more breaths, sat up on the floor and coughed again.

"Studying helps a bit on the way to knowledge. Still, nothing beats practical experience."

"Of what?" John exclaimed in an upset voice. "Of playing some kind of fakir and scaring people out of their minds?"

Sherlock waved deprecatingly and looked up on the woman in the lab coat.

"So, Carol—what did it look like?"

The woman instead turned to John, shook his hand and said politely:

"Carol Blackmore, assistant at the Victoria Mortuary. Sherlock asked me to help out at this experiment and to let you in through the front door. Excuse me for not being so talkative earlier. I didn't want to leave him here without supervision longer than necessary."

By now Sherlock had pulled himself up to sitting position. The pain in muscles and joints seemed to affect him considerably.

"I'm sorry if the experience was too much of a shock to you, John. But Carol here doesn't have enough experience of medical tests. Well, on living people, I mean . . . That's why I needed you here right now."

"But why not just explain things, so I could come here in good time before six o' clock?" John asked, both surprised and irritated.

"Dear friend, it wouldn't have been of much help if you'd come earlier. I had decided to hang on the bar for fifteen minutes, and thereafter document how this affected my body. But seventeen minutes were more than enough, I can assure you. My goodness, what excruciating pain towards the end!"

He rolled his shoulders and looked up towards John again. "So, what were the test results?"

"Well, from my point of view quite what I would have expected. Your pulse and blood pressure was higher than normal, like in ordinary exercise. Now, I can't perform a full blood analysis with such limited equipment, but from what I had . . . "

John looked over the test material he'd received from Carol. "Well . . . The level of lactic acid has gone up considerably, while the carbon dioxide level in your blood has fallen."

"Any idea of what would have happened if I could have carried on?"

John responded, clinically: "It would have been more and more difficult for the heart to pump blood to your brain, and the breathing problems would have increased. The levels of lactic acid and carbon dioxide would probably have continued in the same direction, with a large risk of loss of consciousness."

"Very interesting," said Sherlock slowly. "That would confirm things."

"But dear, incomprehensible Sherlock!" John cried out. "Why in the world such a completely grotesque exercise? What did you plan to achieve by this?"

"As I said, literature is good for a lot of things. But I felt that I also had to do what I could—without risking my life—to get at least a glimpse of the experience."

"The experience of . . . ?"

"Crucifixion."

John Watson closed his eyes, shook his head and struggled to reign in his racing thoughts. He sighed and looked back in Sherlock's by now quite animated eyes.

"Crucifixion?"

"I can proudly report that we've come at least a bit further in this case," Sherlock smiled triumphantly.

John looked slightly irritated. "Well, imagine that I was foolish enough to imagine a visit to the local mortuary as part of a more . . . shall we say . . . 21st century inquiry."

"The night isn't over yet, my friend! We have bodies yet to examine. But the goal isn't to investigate their specific causes of death. Our case concerns Jesus of Nazareth, who was executed on a cross, and therefore completely—dead. Marvellous!" Sherlock took a few deep breaths, rose and laid his arm on John's shoulder. "And how does my dear doctor look upon this issue, based on the research you have been doing during the last week?"

John felt slightly embarrassed. Yes, he had actually spent an hour or so surfing the net and out of sheer curiosity looking over the vast amount of speculations surrounding the death of Jesus. He soon felt that the topic was too distant, though, with too many strange alternatives to spend his time on.

"To be honest, I haven't put in as much effort as you, neither theoretically, nor . . . practically." Once again he looked up towards the bar in the ceiling. "What I did note was that there appears to be tons of suggestions of what might have happened to Jesus. As a doctor, I obviously realize how unlikely it would be for somebody to survive such a barbaric execution as a crucifixion. But considering the amount of explanations, perhaps there may actually be some alternative answer?"

"Then I'll gladly be your guide through a Roman crucifixion in Jerusalem somewhere around year 30 after . . . well, basically after the birth of our victim in question."

Sherlock bent down and picked up his long coat from the floor, and with some difficulty put it on. "I suggest we now turn to a couple of present-day corpses, and thereafter continue this conversation over a cup of tea. Carol, would you mind letting us into the cold-storage room?"

CHAPTER 4

LOOKING DEATH IN THE EYE

CAROL BLACKMORE HAD WORKED at the mortuary for two years. She'd hesitated more than once before she applied for the job. It didn't take very long, though, before she got used to the job of bringing in and preparing dead bodies for funeral, without feeling too personally affected by the daily business.

Every now and then she also got to assist doctors and police investigators who visited the mortuary in order to establish causes of death. It was on one such occasion that she first became acquainted with the lanky man in the coat. He did seem quite introverted, thought Carol at the time, but still pretty charming when he made an effort. She didn't remember exactly how, but somehow he had managed to convince her to let him in through the side entrance after closing hours when he wished to examine something particular on some corpse. Each time he had been very polite, no indecent behaviour in any way. A little strange, maybe, but never intimidating or threatening.

This time Sherlock Holmes had an unusual request when she had let him in: to be strung up by leather straps onto the metal bar hanging from the ceiling at 17:45. If the situation had been different, she would have felt discomforted and immediately sent the visitor back out. But something in Sherlock's conduct made her calm, despite the odd request. Suspended up there, he'd asked Carol to fetch a friend at the entrance at exactly 18:00 and then return as soon as possible.

"I apologize for the discomfort I may have caused by coming a bit late, said John quietly to Carol as she pulled out her access card to get into the cold-storage room.

"Not at all," she answered in a low voice. "I understand if you were a bit shaken by the experience down here."

"Oh, I'm quite used to things like these," mumbled John and followed her into the chilly room.

John looked at the thermometer on the wall. Seven degrees centigrade. He compared his own jacket to Sherlock's lined coat, and decided that he didn't want to stay in here longer than necessary. Sherlock looked around and said:

"Well then, let's look at some examples of wounds. Have you arranged the bodies in the order I asked for?"

Water vapour came from Sherlock's mouth as he spoke. He glanced at Carol who nodded at the closest stretcher.

"Here is a corpse with a stab wound in his chest, just as you requested."

"Brilliant," answered the detective contentedly and pulled away the cover from face and body.

†

An hour later John sank down in an armchair in the café on the opposite side of the street from the mortuary. There could hardly be two places with more opposing atmospheres than these, he thought to himself, while Sherlock with some pains put two cups of tea on the table, and sat himself down in the other armchair.

"Now, may I get your initial reaction to this evening's exercises?" asked Sherlock curiously.

"I still can't help but wonder about the purpose behind putting yourself through something so insane as voluntarily hanging yourself up on a metal bar?"

"You've never been to the gym, John?" Sherlock smiled. "People pay huge amounts of money to torture their bodies for a little while. For me, though, the intention was to get a practical insight into at least a fraction of what a crucifixion does to the human body."

"So what was it like?" John lifted up his cup and put it carefully in his lap.

"Absolutely terrible. Worst was the pain across my shoulders, which had to carry more or less my whole body weight." Sherlock took a sip from his tea, leaned forward and almost whispered: "But that's of course just a drop in the ocean, compared to the indescribable torment that a real Roman crucifixion would inflict."

"I'm not really certain that I want to hear this, but . . . you've studied the whole execution procedure in an equally zealous manner?"

Sherlock lit up. "Dear friend, I thought you'd never ask! Here's the case: There is a number of Roman sources that describe crucifixions in general. There are also some extra-biblical descriptions of this execution method in contemporary Palestine, most notably from Josephus."

"And he was . . . ?" wondered John.

"Josephus was a Jewish historian who defected to the Roman side." Sherlock lowered his voice slightly: "He and other sources recount a truly bestial punishment, used on people that the Romans wished to humiliate and torture to death in the worst possible way."

John shuddered, and thought of news headlines about how modern terrorist groups had gone so far as to crucify their victims. He had refused to look at the pictures, but just the thought gave him a strong sense of unease. Sherlock seemed to be able to read his thoughts, and continued: "There is actually also some more current research on how a crucifixion affects the human body. Completely voluntary experiments, I might add. Among these is an American forensic scientist who's conducted experiments by suspending volunteers in different positions in order to see what happened to their bodies."[1]

Sherlock took a pause to massage his shoulders, and then continued with the Roman method of execution: "Sometimes ropes were used to fasten the crucified to the cross. In other cases, the Romans fastened them with nails, between five and seven inches long. These were usually hammered in through the victim's wrists and feet."

John felt cold waves running down his spine. By now he'd forgotten all about his teacup.

"It really feels quite unpleasant to sit here and talk about these things, but . . . isn't Jesus traditionally pictured with nails through his palms instead?"

Sherlock shook his head. "This doesn't seem to have been the standard practice.

---

1. The scientist's name is Frederick Zugibe, and his experiments (which were more advanced versions of the experiment that Sherlock in this story performs on himself) plus conclusions may be found in the film *How Jesus Died—the Final 18 Hours* (Shotgun Pictures 1995) or at http://www.crucifixion-shroud.com/experimental_studies_in_crucifix.htm

He continued, with a smile: "There are others out there too, who have tried practical ways of examining lethal violence to the body. There was a French physician who experimented on an amputated arm, where he nailed the palm to a surface and then hung half the bodyweight of a normal man on the other end of the arm. This way he wanted to see whether the palm would be able to support the load of a crucifixion."

"And the result?" asked John.

"The hand couldn't bear the weight for more than ten minutes," Sherlock stated. "Together with other reasons, this leads me to the conclusion that the nails probably were hammered in through the wrists."[2]

Still filled with the pictures of the dead bodies from the mortuary only a few minutes ago, John wished for more concrete evidence: "But are there no preserved remains from crucified persons that one could study?"

Sherlock rubbed his hands in excitement, while continuing his lecture: "Archaeologists searched for a long time for such remains from the time around Jesus, but never managed to find any. Mainly because the bodies often were left on the cross to rot. In some cases, however, the Romans gave the family permission to bury the victim. In later years the remains of a crucified man have actually been discovered. And as if by sheer coincidence he was found in—Jerusalem!"

"How about that!" John smiled back. "And if there was the slightest possibility that it might have been Jesus . . . "

"Then we would most certainly have heard it on the news," laughed Sherlock. "No, the gravesite actually reveals the identity of the victim. His name was Yehohanan, son of Hagkol.[3] We know he was crucified because there's still a nail left through the heel bone. Interestingly, there was also a small piece of olive tree left from where the feet were fastened."

John couldn't help feeling a bit distressed at this concrete information. He quickly regained a professional attitude: "Did this finding give any closer indications of how the crucifixion was executed?"

2. The doctor was Pierre Barbet. His results, which showed that a nail fastened in the middle of the palm would tear through the hand, can be found in his book *A Doctor at Calvary*. Whether this experiment actually gave the correct picture of the procedure is contested by Frederick Zugibe and others, not least because the victims could rest some bodyweight on the small footstep on which the victim's feet were usually fastened in Roman crucifixions.

3. The remains of Yehohanan were discovered at a building site in Jerusalem in 1968. He is estimated to have been crucified some time during the first century AD, i.e. very close to Jesus in both a geographical and a historical sense.

"Yes, in some ways. You can't tell from the skeleton exactly how the arms were fastened to the cross. What you can see, though, is that his legs have been broken, just like the gospels and other sources state was modus operandi at crucifixions."[4]

"I don't think I follow," John protested. "Was it customary to torture the dying even more when they were hanging on the cross?"

"On the contrary, John." Sherlock once more tried with pain to move his shoulders. "The reason I could manage hanging on the bar for as long as I did was that I could rest a little bit of the body weight on my toes. The same thing applied for those who were crucified during antiquity; their feet were usually fastened to a small footrest. In order to shorten their suffering, the Romans used to crush the legs on the dying victims. The result of this was that they could no longer use the legs to raise themselves up in position to breathe. Instead, they had to pull themselves up by the arms to inhale and exhale. Nobody can manage this for more than a few minutes in that condition. Then it's all over."

Man is truly capable of the most hideous acts, reflected John. Both now and then. The feeling of nausea crept up within him. He did manage, though, to push away the unpleasant images from his head, and tried to collect his thoughts.

"So what conclusions should we draw from Yehohanan's case, in relation to our own?"

"Well, obviously it strengthens the information in the gospels about the nails, the crushing of bones—in short: the crucifixion as such," Sherlock answered, seemingly emotionally undisturbed by the horrific scenes that they had just discussed.

John lifted his teacup to his lips. The tea had become cold.

"OK, perhaps we shouldn't dwell on it," he said. "But I've read a number of alternative theories on what might have happened to Jesus. Perhaps he drank a magic potion that made him only appear to die. Perhaps he was replaced by a double. And so on."

Sherlock smiled indulgently. "John, we're both rational people. But these conspiracy theorists seem to be everywhere. Almost every time a

---

4. See for example Koskenniemo, Erkki; Nisula, Kirsi; Toppari, Jorma "Wine Mixed with Myrrh (Mark 15.23) and Crurifragium (John 19.31–32): Two Details of the Passion Narratives" in *Journal for the Study of the New Testament*, June 2005 27: 379–391. Web version at http://jnt.sagepub.com/content/27/4/379.full.pdf+html It should be added that John 19:33 explains that Jesus' bones were not crushed, as he was already dead when the soldiers crushed the bones of the other two crucified men.

well-known person meets sudden death, crazy ideas like these turn up. And they're always accompanied by one common feature: a complete lack of evidence. I suggest that we proceed as we do in all other cases: Gather as many reliable facts as possible, and from there, we draw our conclusion. And when nuts show up: ignore them."

John still wasn't entirely satisfied. "Hang on a second, remember there are millions of Muslims in the world. Don't they have the idea that God in some way pulled Jesus up to heaven, and then another man was crucified in his place."

Sherlock replied with a tired look: "Dear John—you're a doctor. What do you say yourself?"

"Well, I don't believe that. But . . . "

"But what?" Sherlock raised his voice. "I don't have anything against religion. People may believe whatever they like as far as I'm concerned. But historical events which can be studied factually, that's another matter. Or what do you think: should we throw all contemporary witness reports in the bin and instead accept some kind of magical solution that somebody claims to have had revealed from heaven six hundred years later?"

John felt a bit ashamed. "I know. But still, this is in the highest degree a religious question, isn't it?

"No, it isn't," replied Sherlock firmly. "The question whether there's a God who has caused this or that—there you have a religious question. On the other hand, whether there was a convicted prisoner named Jesus of Nazareth who was executed through crucifixion—this is a perfectly scientific question. And when dealing with this question I definitely feel safer with historical facts than with supernatural magic."

John could see Sherlock's point. He was glad that his companion used his regular methods even in a case as strange as this one.

"I guess this leaves us with the question whether we can be absolutely certain that Jesus died on the cross?"

"A quite central point, isn't it?" Sherlock cried enthusiastically and rose with some agony. "I suggest that we wait a moment with that detail. Let's leave and take the tube back to Baker Street."

CHAPTER 5

DEATH ON A CROSS

It didn't take many minutes before the two men had rushed through London's underground system and found themselves back home again. During the short trip back, John's thoughts had spun around the bewildering events down in the domains of the mortuary. He had also tried to get a grip of how Sherlock's personal experiments related to a very real crucifixion outside the walls of Jerusalem some two thousand years ago. Sherlock had left John alone with his thoughts during the journey, focusing his own attention on massaging his aching shoulders.

John made himself comfortable in the armchair, and decided to return to where they had left off some minutes ago:

"So, let's hear now: Did Jesus die on the cross, or is there any room for uncertainty?"

With some effort Sherlock got seated in the sofa.

"Ouch . . . Not that I was really close to death down there, but damn it how it affected muscles and joints." Sherlock pulled himself together and continued:

"It was important for me to spend time up there on the bar. Breathing was obviously laboured, but most difficult was the pain, even when I rested a bit of my weight on the footrest. Already after five minutes, the pain started to become almost more than I could bear. But I still wished to carry on long enough to get an idea of how my body was affected. What it would have felt like after one or even a couple of hours more, I dare not even think about," Sherlock grinned.

"So I guess death would have been a liberation for someone who was crucified?"

"Without a doubt. You and I have encountered several present-day criminals with a rather lively imagination when it comes to ways of tormenting other people. But the Romans really created a death penalty so diabolic that it has hardly been surpassed in cruelty." Sherlock took a short pause to think: "Now remember that the victims—just like Jesus—first had been severely flogged, lost a lot of blood, and hereby also suffered from a terrible thirst. In addition to this, they usually had to carry the crossbeam to the place of execution. By then, the convicted men were beside themselves with pain and exhaustion, and this at the time when the crucifixion itself hadn't even begun!"

"Frightful!" Even in the secure environment of their own flat, John felt the unease coming over himself once again.

"I admit that you seem to have done some serious delving into this subject," he said. "You mentioned that remains have been discovered of a crucified man in Jerusalem. Something that would be really interesting is if there are any reports of people who were crucified, but for some reason still managed to survive."

"I've done some research on that theme as well!" Sherlock rubbed his hands in amusement that the conversation went on in precisely the direction he wanted. "Josephus actually describes an occasion where he happened to spot three men who had just been crucified, and realized that they were personal acquaintances of his.[5] He became so infuriated that he immediately asked the officer on duty to take the three men down."

"Were they fastened by nails or rope?" asked John.

"Unfortunately, Josephus doesn't mention this. Neither does he write how long they had hung on the crosses. So we don't know exactly how badly affected the victims were when they were removed. But as soon as they were taken down, they were given immediate medical care."

"And how quickly did they regain their health?" wondered John.

Sherlock made a rhetorical pause, and answered: "This is a very important insight: The medical staff actually managed to save the life of one of them. The other two, though, had suffered such serious injury that they died anyway, even though they were saved from the cross and afterwards given the best care available."

---

5. Episode described in Josephus *The life of Flavius Josephus*; 75.

John hummed, in some surprise: "I guess this means that we can be sure that any person who was hung on a cross normally did so all the way until death?"

Sherlock nodded. "That's the best conclusion we can draw, based on the information we have about Roman crucifixions. Besides, the soldiers had a very basic mission: to make sure that the convict actually died. It was also in their own interest not to leave a victim hanging there longer than necessary; they wanted to complete their job so they could get back to their barracks. And part of this task was to remain on the spot of the execution until they were certain that their victims were dead."[6]

Most parts of the world had indeed become somewhat more civilized since antiquity, John mused silently.

"I've been thinking a bit as a professional too," John added with some pride in his voice. Sometimes it felt as if Sherlock completely forgot that John had any professional competence concerning the human body. "Based on what you've told me tonight, I get the impression that it should have been quite evident to everybody when a person had died on the cross. If the bones were crushed to shorten the suffering, and the victims thereby needed to pull themselves up by the arms in order to get some air, then everyone would be able to declare the moment of death when . . . "

"Exactly," interrupted Sherlock. "When the dying no longer found the strength to pull themselves up to breathe.[7] By the way, the apostle John also states another detail about the death of Jesus, which he claims to have seen personally," the detective added.[8]

---

6. The function of the Roman soldiers, as well as the entire procedure of crucifixion is described in many sources, for instance Retief, F P & Cilliers, L "The history and pathology of crucifixion" *The South African Medical Journal* 2003; 93: 938–941. Web version at http://www.samj.org.za/index.php/samj/article/viewFile/2462/1710

7. There are several hypotheses on the actual cause of death of crucifixion victims. Some suggest cardiac rupture, hypovolemic shock or asphyxia, or perhaps some combination of lack of oxygen, dehydration and other indirect causes of death. Zugibe rejects the traditional explanation of asphyxia as a consequence of the victims no longer being able to pull themselves up to breathe, because his test subjects did not experience such serious breathing problems. On the other hand, these persons had to quit the experiment after a rather short time, due to the severe pain. It is therefore unknown exactly how great the breathing difficulties would have been after a couple of hours.

A good summary of this topic is found in Maslen, Matthew W & Mitchell, Piers D "Medical Theories on the Cause of Death in Crucifixion" *Journal of the Royal Society of Medicine* April 2006 vol. 99 no. 4 185–188. Electronic version at http://jrs.sagepub.com/content/99/4/185

8. John 19:31–35

"When Friday evening approached, the Jewish leaders wished to speed up the process so that no bodies would be left on the crosses during the Sabbath. But when the Roman soldiers were to crush the bones of the dying in order to hasten death, they realized that Jesus was already dead. Here John also gives the extra information that one soldier confirmed Jesus' death, by . . . "

" . . . by thrusting a spear into his side!" John interrupted, suddenly blushing with anger. "An outrageous practice. I've seen similar in the war fields. You demonstrate once and for all that an enemy has died, while at the same time desecrating his body."

Somewhat surprised by his friend's strong reaction, Sherlock continued calmly: "Well, the main purpose of the procedure wasn't to desecrate, but to get a final verification that death had arrived. It wasn't used at every execution, but it was still a common way to end a crucifixion."[9]

The detective started to look a bit puzzled: "But one thing that strikes me as a bit odd in the information about the spear in the side is the description of what came out. Blood and water. How would you explain this, John?"

The ex-army doctor leaned back in his armchair and replied: "Water rarely appears in pure form in the human body. Normally, it's mixed in the blood, especially in the plasma. Though when you separate this from the blood cells, the plasma does look like water. This also appears a short time after a person's death, though it doesn't take long before everything coagulates. So if the description is correct, it may have been another verification that Jesus had died just moments ago."

Sherlock folded his arms with some reservation.

"So that's your solution to the "blood-and-water-description"?

John thought for some more, and then answered: "Well, if we think one step further, there may be another explanation."

Sherlock lit up. "Now you're speaking my language! If you lift up another stone, you often come across a new hypothesis that may be of use. Let's hear!"

"In that case, I think I'd need you to stand up. Then I can illustrate."

Sherlock rose willingly, while John came up to him on the other side of the table.

9. This procedure is described by Roman author Quintilian, who wrote a few years after the crucifixion of Jesus. See his *Declarationes maiores* 6:9, referred to in Habermas, Gary & Licona, Michael *The Case for the Resurrection of Jesus* (Kregel Publications 2004) p 102.

"Now, could you please raise your arms?"

"You don't think I've had enough of these positions tonight?" remarked Sherlock with a restrained chuckle.

"This will only take a moment. Let's imagine that you're being crucified, and I'm the Roman soldier." John squatted down beside Sherlock. The detective grinned in agony:

"I'm sorry, John. My arms feel like lead," he moaned and let his arms fall.

"That's alright. Now, if I were to pierce your side with a spear, then it should enter your body about . . . here," John explained and let his finger point diagonally upwards in front of Sherlock's hanging arm, and in at about the middle of his left side.

"Sounds highly plausible," commented Sherlock. "And if your spear would reach a bit further into my body, then you'd reach . . . ?"

"Then I'll soon reach your lung."

"Ah—that's what I thought!" exclaimed Sherlock and took the liberty of sitting down again. "And now for the really interesting thing: what comes out then?"

"In this case, for a victim who had suffered hours of extreme torture, finally leading to his death, then the lung sack and to some extent also the heart sack start to be filled with water. If a sharp object were to penetrate the body through the lung and into the heart a short time after the moment of death, you would see blood and something similar to water coming out from the wound."

Sherlock placed his elbows on the armrests, put his fingertips together and summarized: "Magnificent! We have combined theory and practice, and we have let modern science cast its light upon past events.[10] I think we have achieved what we needed tonight."

"I might just add," John continued, "that I obviously don't have a clue whether this spear would have come in from left or right. Neither do I know whether the description might refer to blood plasma or lung fluid."

"No, and this is not central to the main question," Sherlock agreed. "Most important is that we seem to have solved the first step in our case. We

10. Edwards, Gabel & Hosmer "On the physical death of Jesus Christ" *Journal of the American Medical Association*, vol 255, No 11, gives a coherent picture of the crucifixion and death of Jesus from a medical perspective. Also at http://www.godandscience.org/apologetics/deathjesus.pdf

may now regard it as an established fact that Jesus of Nazareth was executed and died on a cross."[11]

John sat silent, and let the fact sink in.

"And then we're stuck with the significant question of what happened afterwards," he mumbled.

Once again, silence fell in the room. But Sherlock soon roused his flatmate from his contemplation of the executed man from Nazareth.

"So, would you care to retell what actually happened in Afghanistan?"

"Oh, right . . . There was one time in Kandahar. Our team didn't make it in time before the massacre was over. And the corpses . . . " John grew silent and looked away, his face filled with disgust.

Sherlock waited politely. John gave a long sigh.

"Nope, having to encounter and deal with desecrated and mutilated bodies isn't anything I long to return to. You know, war does something horrible to a person's mind. Both for those who commit the deeds, and for those who have to witness the result."

His brow wrinkled as he did a quick mental review of future career choices: "No. I think it will have to be a quite ordinary doctor's practice for me in the future. I'm done with the army."

Sherlock thought for a moment, and then decided to knit together the present and the past:

"You know, John. I can imagine that your reaction may be quite similar to how the closest followers of Jesus might have experienced his death. To them, though, it was more than an executed body to take care of. They must have felt as if their whole world fell apart, when the man they thought would liberate them was captured, tortured and then brutally killed before their eyes. Can you imagine how that must have been?"

"Yeah . . . " murmured John. "It must have been a shattering psychological experience. All their Messianic dreams crushed in just one day. From triumphant entry in Jerusalem to complete disaster in less than a week."

"Precisely," Sherlock continued. "It's quite hard to imagine more devastated people than those who late Friday afternoon helped each other to take down Jesus' dead body and bury it."

---

11. Jesus' death on the cross is almost completely unquestioned among contemporary scholars. Bart Ehrman, a critical scholar who does not accept the resurrection, lists in his book *Did Jesus Exist?* no less than eleven independent sources which describe that Jesus died through crucifixion.

John nodded slowly and turned his eyes to the window. The evening was late, and there was no cloud in the London sky. A full moon had just come up over the rooftops. One lunar month left until Easter, thought John. Could it be possible in such a short amount of time to find a solution to a problem such as this?

With some difficulty Sherlock got up and put an end to the discussion:

"It's been a long and fruitful evening. But now I need to rest my strained limbs. And I guess you have a blog to write?"

"Not now . . . " answered John thoughtfully. "This issue actually feels a bit too odd to share with the public. At least right now."

The two men turned off the lights and entered their separate bedrooms. The moon cast its glow through the window, brightly lighting some parts of the deserted room. Though large parts still remained in deep shadow.

Chapter 6

A KNOWN GRAVE

Morning came, and John Watson got up to make some breakfast. He soon realized that Sherlock was already gone. Well then, better to let him work according to his own fashion and time-table, John figured. The sun was shining from the blue London sky, and he decided to have breakfast outdoors. John went down to the closest café and bought a breakfast bag, which he took with him into Regent's Park.

He sat down on a bench, unpacked the simple breakfast, and took a sip of smoking hot coffee through the hole in the plastic cover of the mug. The spring morning was chilly, though beautiful. John closed his eyes and enjoyed the moment.

"What is the simplest way to find a grave?" A familiar voice broke the silence from behind.

"Sherlock!" John started at the unexpected appearance.

"Oh, it wasn't my intention to scare you," the newcomer excused himself, came around and sat down beside his flatmate. "I've just been on a brief morning trip."

"Yes, so I noted. And you've been to . . . ?"

"The cemetery."

"Well, I should have guessed . . . I hope you haven't practiced being buried alive today?" smiled John and took a first bite of his sandwich.

"Morning humour, much appreciated!" Sherlock smiled and gave him a friendly nudge in his side. "No, cemeteries are good places in many ways—especially if you want some peace and quiet to think. But back to my question: How do you go about locating a certain person's grave?"

John felt a need to first get a hold of where the discussion was heading:

"Is this about the same thing as last night, or about something completely different?"

"Well, I guess the question concerns more or less all such cases. But let's say you wanted to visit a famous person's grave; how do you proceed?"

John put his hand into his pocket and quickly pulled out his phone.

"Google!" he answered triumphantly.

"Ok, let's say you do that. You would then get the information that Winston Churchill—just to name someone—lies buried in a family tomb in Oxfordshire. That's common knowledge. But when you get to the church in question, how do you find his particular grave?"

"I guess I'll ask a cemetery worker."

"Splendid! I enjoyed myself with practising just this method an hour ago. Cemetery workers are early birds. Not always very talkative, but they often know their cemetery as well as the back of their own hand. It's stunning how easily they can find the tombs of almost every person, famous or unknown. But let's say the workers have a day off—how do you find the correct tomb in that case?"

"Well, if there's no guiding sign, I would probably look for somebody else that seemed to know the place."

"Very good; if plan A fails, you turn to plan B. I did that this morning, just to check, and realized that even the average cemetery visitor is surprisingly well-informed when it comes to other people's graves. Well, at least as long as I asked for a well-known figure."

"And how does this lead us closer to the answer to our historic riddle?" wondered John.

"The interesting thing about people is that they seem to behave quite similarly, regardless of era. Which brings us back to our case: Where would you find Jesus' tomb?"

John tried to recall. He had never visited the Holy Land, but he vaguely remembered having seen some pictures.

"Isn't there some kind of rock tomb preserved?"

"Oh yes, there is a place called the Garden Tomb. Still, that mainly appears to be some kind of scam to attract tourists. There seems to be no evidence that Jesus was buried there. No, the general belief is that the gravesite itself is located within the Church of the Holy Sepulchre in Jerusalem. But this is still merely a conjecture. We don't know for certain the exact location where Jesus was buried."[12]

"Hm . . . " said John and took the last sip of his coffee. "Doesn't this mean that this case seems more or less unsolvable?" he asked, almost hopefully.

"By no means," Sherlock answered with an enthusiastic smile. "The crucial question is: was the grave site known to the public a short time after the crucifixion or not?"

John opened a bottle of orange juice and sifted through his memories. "Didn't you say that those who were crucified were considered so low that they were usually left on the cross after death?"

"Exactly. Others were just thrown into a pit after death. In those circumstances there was no tomb to visit at all. But those treatments don't fit with what we know in this particular case."

"Just a moment," John interrupted. "You said *know*. But this is surely a matter of faith, not science! You really seem to have been talking a bit too much with church folks lately."

"An important remark, my friend." Sherlock patted him on the shoulder in a friendly fashion. "We're not dealing with any matters of faith whatsoever here. But we need to find out what historic facts we can claim to *know*, before we can draw any conclusions on what we still *don't* know. Allow me to illustrate!"

Sherlock got up and searched on the ground around the park bench. Soon he'd picked up an empty beer can.

"What is this?"

"A can of Carlsberg, obviously. An empty one too, as far as I can tell."

"Exactly. This we *know*. But who has been drinking from this can? Why has it been thrown here? Where was it bought? These are a number of questions that we still haven't found the answers to. Now let's say that we weren't down here, but up in our own flat. If Mrs Hudson then came up and told us angrily that she'd seen an empty can of Carlsberg next to a bench in Regent's Park—would you believe her?"

John thought for a moment. Was it a trick question? He decided to be forthright:

12. However, recent research at the site provides even stronger evidence that the shrine called the *Edicule* in the Church of the Holy Sepulchre, may very well be the tomb where Jesus was buried after his death. See Romey, Kristin "Exclusive: Age of Jesus Christ's Purported Tomb Revealed" *National Geographic* 11/2017, https://news.national-geographic.com/2017/11/jesus-tomb-archaeology-jerusalem-christianity-rome/

"Yes—I guess I would believe her. Especially if she named the label of the beer can. She wouldn't have any reason to lie about something like that, would she?"

"Excellent!" exclaimed Sherlock. "John, you need to understand: my daily work depends on the possibility of getting reliable testimonies from people. One thing I've noted is that people normally tell the truth in simple matters, if they don't have a particular reason to lie. Though in the latter case their motives for deception usually become apparent quite soon. Therefore, we could probably dare to claim that we *know* that there's an empty beer can next to this park bench, even if we hadn't been here to see it ourselves."

John couldn't but agree that this was the only possible way to reason when doing research. During his own university studies he'd had a couple of fellow students of the super-sceptical kind. They questioned everything, doubted everything. Well, at least they gave that impression. He'd noticed one interesting thing about them, though. When they got into more serious medical work, they became more inclined to accept and base their actions on the factual information they received, even when this came without water-tight evidence.

"You mean that as we don't have a grave left to visit, we need to examine the sources to find out whether there were any testimonies about a known grave at the time of the events?"

"Exactly! That's how all historians work, by the way. In this case—as in all others—we need to know what we know. Without facts we just wander around helplessly with mere guesses. That won't do. Therefore, I'm determined to find out what facts we can establish about the events in Jerusalem at the time in question 2000 years ago."

"Yes, wasn't it the Jewish Passover that week-end?"

"That's correct. And that was one of the reasons why the bodies couldn't be left hanging on the crosses when Friday evening approached. It was somehow considered to defile the coming Sabbath and Passover feast." Sherlock looked down on the ground: "Well, I'm obviously no expert in this field, even if I've taken quite some time to study these events."[13]

John took the last bite of his sandwich and returned to the main question:

"So, what do we know about the burial of Jesus?"

---

13. For studies in Jewish burial practices around the time of Jesus, see for example Craig, William Lane "Assessing the New Testament Evidence for the Historicity of the Resurrection of Jesus" *Studies in the Bible and Early Christianity* 16 (2002)

"Well, we don't know for sure where the exact burial site was. But *who* performed the burial we know with great certainty."

John tried to remember. It was some kind of low-profile figure, he recalled.

"The apparently self-proclaimed undertaker was Joseph of Arimathea," Sherlock said before John could come up with the name.

"Right, that guy!" John's face lit up. "I think I've read some intriguing myths about him." John's suddenly looked worried. "Please, don't say that you've started to believe in old legends?"

Sherlock giggled a bit: "You mean the story that Joseph and Jesus attempted to stage a of coup after the crucifixion, found a boat and set off up here to our nation? *And did those feet in ancient time walk upon England's mountains green?* No, these legends are obviously pure drivel. You can't help feeling a bit ashamed as an Englishman that this tune has had such success, as it's built entirely on historical nonsense," Sherlock muttered.

John looked relieved. "Ok, but you still mean that there's a historical core of truth concerning the person Joseph himself?"

"This is where it gets interesting. You know there are four accounts of Jesus of Nazareth?"

"Matthew, Mark, Luke and John, right?"

"Yep. The first three have many things in common, but after the death of Jesus all four give quite different details. But there is one piece of information that appears in all four gospels: the one about this Joseph burying Jesus in a rock tomb, and afterwards rolling a stone in front of the entrance."

John still felt a bit sceptical: "You know, I think we may have a central issue for the whole case here. I'm not saying that this information is spurious. But the gospels were written by Christians, not by neutral bystanders. I mean, why should we rely on anything they say?"

"John, have you ever met a person that's completely neutral?" Sherlock gave a short laugh. "I meet people all the time who want to describe their version of a given situation. Some of them are incredibly engaged in the matter. But that doesn't automatically mean that they don't tell the truth. The vital question is—both today and two thousand years ago—whether or not we have good reason to think that people give incorrect information."

John frowned as he continued: "But surely we must be able to criticize the gospels as a quite peculiar kind of source material. After all, they're documents of faith, rather than strict biographies."

A smile spread across Sherlock's face. "Well done, John! I actually thought exactly that way when we entered this project. But since then, I've had time to study some current research on ancient biographies. And it turns out that the gospels have the same basic outline as common Greco-Roman biographies.[14] And that's one of the reasons we may also treat them with the same kind of critical scrutiny as we do with other historical documents."

John murmured, agreeing: "That makes sense. So what should we say then about this Joseph of Arimathea?"

"I'd say that this piece of information has the typical characteristics of a reliable description. People or events who are mentioned just briefly, but still so clearly identifiable that a contemporary reader would easily be able to check the information—such statements are almost never made up."

"You mean that a more fanciful rendition would begin 'Once upon a time . . .'"

"Yes. But in our case here, we have four different authors that describe the burial in slightly different words, but they all give the same basic facts. That indicates that this description of Jesus' burial was commonly accepted at the time after the crucifixion."

John wiped his mouth one last time with his napkin. He still wasn't completely ready to let the discussion come to a close.

"But why a man from the same group that had just sentenced Jesus to death?"

"Yes, it certainly seems a little odd. The only writer who gives a clue is Luke—who by the way was a physician by occupation."

"I like him already!" smiled John, though with a touch of irony.

"Luke states that Joseph hadn't agreed to the decision to kill Jesus," continued Sherlock.[15] "He might have voted nay, he might have been absent from the meeting. We don't know. But the fact that a familiar figure is described as having taken care of the burial would obviously have made the Christian story completely absurd from the very beginning, if such a man hadn't existed!"

---

14. For more information on this topic: see Burridge, Richard A. *What are the gospels? A comparison with Greco-Roman Biography* (Eerdmans 2004 (2nd revised edition)) This is most probably the book that has had the largest impact on this research.

15. Luke 23:51

"Well, I don't know if that would be sufficient for us today," John figured. "People have an amazing ability to come up with the most outrageous stories."

" . . . about things that nobody can check!" Sherlock interrupted. "In those situations people show an enormous creativity. Though it's very unusual that people lie about details where someone may actually call their bluff."

Sherlock leaned closer on the bench and said in a low voice: "However, what's truly fascinating is what the greatest critics of Christianity said about alternative grave sites."

John looked bewildered. "I thought that there were no rumours at all about any alternative tomb?"

Sherlock leaned back again with a pleased look on his face. "And that, John, is precisely what's so interesting. Not *a single one* of the early critics of the Christian faith put forward any such suggestion."[16]

John thought intensely, and in the meantime he rolled up what was left of his breakfast bag into a ball. He decided to try to follow Sherlock's train of thought.

"So you mean that . . . as no critics suggested any other grave site, we may deduce that . . . " John took a moment's pause. Sherlock didn't fill it, so he continued: " . . . that all parties agreed on the site of Jesus' tomb?"

"Bravo!" Sherlock's smile widened a bit more. "Now, I don't think I can emphasize this enough. After Jesus' crucifixion, the location of the tomb was well-known in Jerusalem to anyone who wanted to investigate things further."[17]

With a satisfied expression, Sherlock threw the beer can into a waste bin across the footpath, and then turned towards his companion.

"So, what do you say? Time to go home?"

He got up from the bench. John followed his example. They started strolling the short way back to the lodgings at Baker Street. Sherlock took the time to complete his lecture:

"Then there are of course a huge number of other hypothetical explanations with a much later historical dating. But these are of small historical value, compared to the descriptions we've just discussed. So, as there are

16. Habermas/Licona *The case for the resurrection of Jesus* p 98

17. John A. T. Robinson, considered as a very liberal theologian, agrees that the burial of Jesus is "one of the earliest and best-attested facts about Jesus." Robinson, John A. T., *The Human Face of God* (Westminster Press 1973) p 131

no contemporary claims that Jesus' body could have been lost, laid in a different tomb or whatever, I think that we may safely assume that Joseph of Arimathea buried Jesus in a readily identifiable grave."[18]

They turned a corner and came towards their own front door. There stood a man who, with an uncertain expression seemed to be trying to make out the name signs next to the door.

"Good morning! Are you searching for anyone in particular?" John greeted the visitor politely.

"I've already been upstairs and knocked on the door, but unfortunately there wasn't anybody home." The stranger stretched out his hand towards John. "Alex Barkley. I'm looking for Mr Sherlock Holmes."

18. New Testament professor Craig Evans concludes: "In my view, much of the scepticism, not to mention the more speculative and improbable theorizing, is due to lack of familiarity with Jewish burial practices. (. . .) What we shall find is that a review of Jewish burial practices, historical documents from late antiquity and archaeological data will provide more than sufficient reason to regard the narratives of the New Testament Gospels as informed, credible historical witnesses. The burial of Jesus, as the Gospels describe it, is a datum of history, not a legend or a hoax." Evans, Craig & Wright, N.T. *Jesus, the Final Days: What Really Happened* (Westminster John Knox Press 2009), p 40–41

CHAPTER 7

THE SCIENCE OF DEDUCTION

SINCE THE BEGINNING OF his acquaintance with Sherlock, John had to the best of his abilities tried to practise some of his methods. He quickly looked over the visitor. He seemed to be in his forties, slightly shorter than John, and with a somewhat stressed appearance. On the other hand, such an appearance was more or less the case with everyone who found their way to 221B Baker Street.

However, it was the detective himself that was the wanted man. John nodded towards his companion.

"Mr Holmes, what great luck that I could find you here!" exclaimed the visitor and shook Sherlock's hand. "I really hope that you are as skilful as people say you are. I have run into a difficult problem at my job, and I . . ."

"At the university or in church?" interrupted Sherlock.

A red flush instantaneously suffused the man's face. "But . . . I don't understand. Has some colleague of mine been here before and asked for your advice?"

"Not at all," Sherlock answered calmly. "It was just a little hard to guess which job you were referring to, since you're both a scholar and a priest."

Alex Barkley stood staring, as if frozen stiff.

"Church of England, if I'm allowed to speculate," Sherlock added. The visitor's eyebrows were now possibly even higher up than before.

"But how . . . ?" he tried, but couldn't manage to complete the sentence.

"Well then, we can't stand down here chatting all day. Let's go upstairs so we can talk more privately," smiled Sherlock and opened the door. "This way, Sir!"

John watched Sherlock's face as he passed him and almost bounced up the stairs. His whole person glowed with what seemed to be a strong pride, as if he'd just won a prestigious award. Sherlock Holmes wasn't normally a vain man, but intellectually he never felt as proud as when he could create this effect. Nothing satisfied him more than when a new acquaintance was astounded by his ability to reveal concealed information about a person.

"May I help you with your coat," asked Sherlock when they had come inside. He put the visitor's outdoor garments on a hanger, and showed him into the flat and the sofa where he could make himself comfortable.

"Well then, I hope that I possess at least part of the competence you require," said Sherlock. He sat down in the armchair opposite, and did his best to look at least a bit disimpassioned. "Some tea?"

The visitor settled himself, adjusted his shirt once or twice and seemed very much disquieted by the situation.

"Well . . . yes . . . A cup of tea would be . . . nice."

John went out into the kitchen to put the kettle on.

"Though I really cannot see how you without even talking to me could figure out not just one, but both my professions?"

"The important thing for now was to find out whether I owned the power of deduction that you required, wasn't it?" Sherlock snapped back. The visitor looked silently down at the floor.

"Alright then," continued the detective. "As we hopefully have that detail sorted out, maybe you would be so kind as to give an account of your business here today."

Alex Barkley cleared his throat and began: "As previously stated . . . well, by you . . . Yes, I'm a priest in the Church of England. A little parish in Hertford, just north of London. Last week a large silver cross disappeared from our church hall." The visitor outlined an object about two feet tall with his hands. "We used to keep it in the church, but because of the . . . well, the risk of theft, we moved it to the church hall, which has better locks and a more advanced alarm system."

Sherlock listened politely. "Now, could you please describe the circumstances around the disappearance?"

"Absolutely. Let me just underline that this is a very old cross. It's belonged to our parish since the 14th century. Scotland Yard have been there. But they have no answers to give, nothing to go on."

Sherlock chuckled in his armchair, seemingly amused, as the guest carried on with his account: "No alarm was set off, and no fingerprints were on the front door or the table where the cross was fastened. Now, this cross is invaluable to our congregation, and it's also a well-known artefact in our county. So when the police couldn't help us, I came here to you."

"You were wise in doing so," mumbled Sherlock slowly, but soon regained the strength in his voice. "I have some hope that the case should be far from impossible to solve. The sad thing is that my colleague Dr Watson and I unfortunately are in the middle of another problem."

"An urgent one, perhaps?" asked the visiting priest, anxiously.

"Well, you can't say that there's any immediate concern that the evidence will disappear!" smiled Sherlock. "The fact is that the missing body actually was lost several centuries ago."

John returned, carrying a tray with three tea cups and some biscuits.

"Why not say it straight out, that you've become absorbed with the events surrounding the death of Jesus of Nazareth himself!" he said, and put the tray down rather brusquely, as if to mark that a bit of respect for the guest's occupation might be in order.

The visitor once again showed signs of great surprise. He took a tea-cup in his hands, thought silently for a moment before he spoke: "This is really . . . very peculiar indeed." Alex Barkley absent-mindedly stirred with the spoon in his cup, before he looked into Sherlock's eyes: "You didn't happen to deduce what academic topic I've chosen in my own research?"

"Well, the only thing I was able to discern was that you seem to have conducted your studies in Scandinavia."

Alex Barkley started a bit, even though he'd now begun to get used to the unfamiliar situation of being known without voluntarily revealing anything about his identity.

"As a matter of fact, that's correct. To be precise, I took my doctoral degree in Denmark. What might be of interest to you, though, is that my main scholarly discipline is New Testament history."

This time it was Sherlock and John who looked at each other with eyebrows raised in surprise.

"Dear me, isn't that the luckiest coincidence!" laughed John.

"Yes, maybe . . . " answered the priest slowly. "Or possibly . . . " He smiled for a second, but soon got a more serious look and returned to business: "So maybe . . . if you, Mr Holmes have the possibility to assist me with our problem, it might be possible for me to be of some assistance with your historical enigma."

Sherlock thought intensely, hands resting on his chin, the fingertips pressed hard against each other. Suddenly he rose to his feet.

"Deal! I do everything in my power to restore the lost cross, and you lend us your expertise in New Testament history. Do we have an agreement?"

The guest nodded, with an exhilarated look on his face. Then he seemed to be struck by an idea; took out his phone and appeared to check something.

"May I ask what your schedule looks like in the near future? I wonder if . . . I shouldn't take you on a little trip."

"Let's see now . . . " With a thoughtful face, Sherlock looked as if he was mentally skimming through a very busy agenda. "Well . . . I have to find a cross. Apart from that we have all the time in the world!"

John drank the last sip of his tea and replied dryly: "You mean that *you* have all the time in the world. You might forget for a second that at least I have some practical details to take care of?"

"Nonsense, John!" Sherlock waved his remark aside. "Neither of us have any indispensable errands for the next days ahead. In this rather singular case we may take things as they come. So right now, I think we can devote a bit of time to digging deeper into this Jerusalem affair."

Sherlock started to collect some stuff from the table. Without looking directly at his new acquaintance, he asked—almost casually:

"And as you're recently divorced, reverend Barkley, maybe you could take some time off to guide us along the way?"

With a gaping mouth the guest once again turned to John, as if to seek for advice. The latter just smiled compassionately, shook his head and shaped his lips to the words: "Let it go." Without commenting Sherlock's remark, John took charge of the situation, cleared his throat and said: "Yes, as Sherlock just said, we would gladly come along on a short journey if it could help us a step further in our quest for answers. But I'm afraid there's neither time nor money for a trip all the way to Jerusalem."

"No, no—I suggest a location much closer to hand. Actually the one spot on earth that has the historically closest connection to the events that you study. Gentlemen, I suggest light luggage."

"We're for warmer latitudes?" wondered John.

"Not really—I hope we could be back already tonight. Let's get dressed and take a walk down to Euston station. From there: the train to Manchester."

†

The train left the station, gained speed, and twenty minutes later it rushed on through the English countryside, lit up by the March sun, which by now had reached its peak in the sky. The three men sat together at a table in the railway carriage. The newcomer had patiently avoided giving voice to the questions that incessantly rushed around in his head. Though finally he had to get some answers:

"Now then, Mr Holmes, would you be so kind as to tell me how you knew all these things about me back there at Baker Street?"

Sherlock calmly adjusted himself in his seat. It was obvious that he loved this situation, to expound before a captive audience how he acquired information that was hidden to everyone else.

"Let's use first names, things are more relaxed that way," he began. "So, Alex—on the whole it was fairly simple. The first thing I noticed when we met outside our front door was the ring you wear on your right hand. When I started my career, I spent quite a bit of time learning to recognize different types of distinctive marks. This knowledge is hugely important when you want to tell a person's identity and place of belonging."

Alex looked a bit embarrassed, took off his ring and handed it over to Sherlock, who lifted it up against the window and examined it carefully.

"If we were to analyse this ring closer, it obviously carries a lot more facts about you. But one immediately apparent piece of information was where in the world you had performed your academic work."

"How is that?" wondered Alex.

"This is a doctor's ring, isn't it?"

The man opposite him nodded.

"Now, this type of doctor´s ring is only used in Scandinavia," Sherlock continued. "It was impossible to tell from a distance exactly which country, but then you were kind enough to tell me yourself that you performed your research in Denmark."

"If it was that easy, I would surely have been able to figure that out for myself," mumbled Alex, and put the ring back on his finger. "This ring did cost some money to get my hands on, I can assure you."

"That's an interesting thing with rings and other jewellery," Sherlock continued aloud, looking out the window on the landscape outside. "They're so expensive to purchase that you rarely take them off, unless there's a good reason." He turned his head and looked Alex directly in the eye. "Isn't that so?"

The learned scholar turned down his eyes, became silent and sort of sunk down in his seat.

"A family issue?" John asked anxiously.

Sherlock carefully took Alex' left wrist and held up his hand in front of himself.

"A ring that's been on a finger for a long time always gives an imprint. The skin becomes smoother and the finger itself a little bit thinner where the ring has been. It's obvious that you for a long time have worn a ring of medium width on your left ring finger, but you don't wear it anymore. The imprint from a ring disappears after a time, but this one still remains. Therefore, it would only have been a short while since you took it off. The time of engagement is rarely long enough for a ring to leave such a distinct mark. Based on these facts, I estimated that you and your wife have just separated."

Sherlock paused, leaned back against the headrest and looked out the window, before he laconically wrapped things up: "Am I right?"

Alex pulled back his hand, sighed, looked up and met John's eyes.

"It's been just over a week since . . . well, yes—since the separation. I hope to God that our marriage won't be lost for good. She . . . I . . . well, probably both of us felt that we've been going round in a destructive dance that didn't lead anywhere. Right now I sleep at our cantor's, while searching for other accommodation."

Thoughtfully, he let the fingers of his right hand move back and forth on the spot where the wedding ring used to be.

"So if you consider that this is my private situation, and on top of that, I've had a burglary on my hands at work—then I think you understand that I find it quite therapeutic to get away on a short trip like this."

John nodded compassionately. He was no therapist, but you could always listen to the hardships of your fellow man, he used to say. Sherlock, on the other hand, was more of a solution-oriented type of guy. Thus, he went on to complete his deduction:

"And when it comes to church matters, Catholic priests don't marry. The removed wedding ring therefore made me guess that you're Anglican."

Alex had begun to get used to Sherlock's cold way of communicating, and confirmed:

"That's correct, I'm an Anglican priest. But one more thing: you still haven't mentioned how you discovered that I'm a priest?"

"The part of a man's clothing that he generally spends the least time on, is also quite often the garment that gives the most information," explained Sherlock, and turned his eyes towards the priest's feet.

"The shoes?" asked Alex, quite surprised. "These are ordinary walking shoes, bought in an ordinary shoe shop."

"Certainly," continued Sherlock. "But the wear and tear of a pair of shoes also reveals something about the actions of the bearer. Now, all shoes get some faint creases across the upper side when they have been used for a while. But if you look here . . . " Sherlock bent down and moved his fingertips across the shoe leather between the toes and the laces. "Here you have a very distinct crease. This signals a person that has spent quite some time on his knees. However, these are no craftman's shoes. Which leaves us with the other possible occupation: priest."

Alex Barkley blushed a little and replied, almost excusing himself:

"Oh . . . Though I have to confess that I'm not really as pious as I might wish. I don't spend that many minutes on my knees each week. Well, with the exception of the last couple of weeks, which have been more difficult than others . . . "

Sherlock gave a smile, which seemed to be at least somewhat sympathetic: "Well, I admit that it was a long shot with the shoes. There was obviously a much stronger card in the deck." Sherlock made a rhetorical pause: "Your shirt. Right now it looks more or less like an ordinary shirt, but on a closer inspection you can see that the collar may be turned into something different. I'd be rather surprised if the inside pocket of your jacket doesn't hide a white piece of cardboard in the shape of a detachable collar, which could turn this piece of garment into a clerical shirt."

Alex didn't reply. He just slowly put his hand inside his jacket and took out the white slip mentioned. "Just a minor correction: they usually come in plastic nowadays . . . But OK—I give up. You really are an amazing observer," he continued, while with a deft hand inserting the collar and hereby changing his clothing into a shirt that signalled the office of a priest.

"Alright then," he continued. "Now as you have revealed most things that might be mentioned about me, I might just as well tell you where we're headed today."

In the same instant a voice came from the speaker system, announcing that the train was approaching its final stop: Manchester Piccadilly.

CHAPTER 8

A FRAGMENT OF TRUTH

THE DISTANCE BETWEEN THE railway station and the final goal provided a refreshing walk of about twenty minutes. The weather had begun to turn cloudy, and a stiff spring breeze blew around the three walkers, who had to pull their outer garments tighter around themselves. They turned a corner and found themselves before a churchlike neo-Gothic building—though without church towers. Alex Barkley halted, turned towards his travel companions and proudly declared:

"Gentlemen—allow me to present The John Rylands Library!"

Sherlock regarded the building with some disdain. "We came all the way to Manchester to visit a library?"

"Not just any library, I can assure you!" declared the priest.

"You've been here before?" John asked.

Alex smiled back. "If you're interested in New Testament history, this is a place you wouldn't want to miss."

They entered the building and came into a grand entrance hall. It didn't take long before a female employee came up and exclaimed:

"Doctor Barkley—how nice to see you again!" She turned to the two men accompanying him. "Have you brought some fellow scholars with you today?"

"I guess you might put it that way!" Alex replied with a smile, turned to John and Sherlock and said in a determined voice: "Alright then, let's take the stairs and begin our studies!"

He led them up a magnificent stone staircase, which brought them into large, quiet stone-floored corridors. The lighting was dim, and the echo of each step disturbed the pervasive silence. The architecture created a subtle atmosphere which didn't inspire to small-talk.

"Maybe we'll have time to see the reading room later," Alex said in a low voice. "There's nothing like it in the world." He lowered his voice almost to a whisper: "But first let me show you something truly exciting."

He slowly opened the door to a side room, where the three men slipped in. Here, the silence was possibly even deeper, the general lighting even more subdued. A single, bright shaft of light was focused upon an exhibition case in the middle of the room. Behind double glass panes they could see a single, small and severely battered piece of something that appeared to be a papyrus or something similar. Without really knowing what they were looking at, a sense of awe came over the two newcomers.

"There it is!" whispered Alex Barkley. The three men cautiously strode forward.

"What we have before us is the world's oldest found fragment from the New Testament," he continued with great solemnity.

They stood for a few seconds and viewed the simple piece of papyrus, not larger than a few square inches.

"What text is it?" asked John in a low voice, while Sherlock circled the exhibition case and discovered that the back of the fragment was also covered with what appeared to be Greek letters.

"As you can see, there's text on both sides," explained Alex, pointing with his finger. "This means that the writing doesn't come from a book scroll, but from a very early codex—an antique type of book—containing the latest of the New Testament gospels, which is the gospel of John."

"More exactly how old is this particular piece?" asked Sherlock.

"This fragment was found in Egypt close to a century ago, and from there it was purchased and placed in this library," explained their guide. "There's a rather strong consensus among scholars that the codex that this fragment comes from was written in the first half of the second century; I would say sometime around 120 AD."[19]

Alex looked at his visitors and lowered his voice again: "Moreover, what's really fascinating is that the gospel of John wasn't written until about

---

19. When dating ancient documents, there is an established method among scholars, called *palaeography*. This means that the dating of documents or mere fragments are based on which writing style was in use at a particular time, a method that has proved to be quite precise. Therefore, scholars agree that this fragment, called *Papyrus P52,* is the world's oldest New Testament handwriting, probably written a few decades after 100 AD.

90 AD or a few years thereafter, which means that the text you see right now would have been written just a few decades after the original text."

"Quite fascinating!" exclaimed Sherlock, though still in a hushed voice.

"If we take things one step further," continued Alex, "the proximity in time becomes even more interesting! The gospel of John was probably written in Ephesus, in modern-day Turkey. The codex that this fragment comes from must first have been written down, and thereafter transported to Egypt, probably by boat. Therefore, it's possible that the fragment before us belongs to the very first generation of handwritings that were copied directly from the original that John himself wrote."

The apostle John's modern namesake wasn't normally a man of emotion. Still, he couldn't help but be moved by the depths of history that this small slip of material represented.

"But what does it say?" he asked, guessing that his comrade didn't have a complete mastery of the original language either. "To us this seems like pure . . . well,"

"Greek, right?" smiled Alex back. "This is actually the reason I brought you here, because the text deals with a particular day in history, which I assume you've already discussed at length. But I suggest that we first move to a place where we may speak in a normal conversational volume."

†

The three men sat down in the library café, and Alex once again took the lead:

"We have now seen the world's oldest handwriting about Jesus of Nazareth. I have to say that I become equally fascinated every time I visit this place and get the opportunity to get this close to the events."

"So what does the little snippet say?" wondered Sherlock, eager to get some help in deciphering the message on the fragment.

"This is really exciting. Both sides of the fragment are from John's eighteenth chapter. The front describes how the Jewish priests demand to Pilate that Jesus must die, and Pilate goes back into his palace and starts to interrogate Jesus."[20]

"Which means that the action takes place just a few hours before the crucifixion!" John exclaimed.

---

20. The fragment does not contain all the words in the text, as it is just part of a page in the codex. However, the number of words and letters is large enough to ascertain that it comes from this specific passage.

"But wait till you hear the message on the opposite side of the fragment." Alex took out his mobile. "Well, you have to excuse me for not reading from a physical Bible. Modern times, you know . . . " he said apologetically. "The back side describes the latter part of Pilate's interrogation of Jesus, and here Jesus changes to a more philosophic reasoning. Here's what the fragment says: 'For this reason I was born, and for this reason I came into the world—to testify to the truth.'" Alex made a short pause, as if to let the message sink in for both himself and his audience. "And then Jesus continues: 'Everyone who belongs to the truth listens to my voice.'"[21]

He looked up to see how his new acquaintances took in the message.

"That hit the nail on the head," mumbled Sherlock. "This is exactly my goal—the truth." He hit the table with his fist and raised his voice. "No hodge-podge speculation or rambling of legend. There must be a way to find out what actually happened!"

"Do you remember how Pilate carries on the discussion?" continued Alex.

John nodded: "He doesn't really answer Jesus, does he?"

"No—he just asks, almost rhetorically: 'What is truth?'[22] Thereafter, he goes out to the crowd and proclaims that he doesn't find Jesus guilty of any crime. And there the text on this fragment ends."

It became quiet around the table. Imagine that this tiny text fragment in Greek, so close in time to the original manuscript, highlights the question of truth, John reflected. Sherlock interrupted his thoughts: "I have another question, now that we have an expert in our little working party. When this fragment was discovered a century or so ago, how well did it match the text in modern Bible editions?"

"A very relevant question," replied Alex. "With the possible exception of a simplification of the expression 'for this', the contents on front and back are actually an exact equivalent to what we have in our current Bibles."[23]

"Now, this also highlights my main attendant question to you as a scholar," continued Sherlock. "The texts that we can read in the New

21. Quotes from John 18:37

22. John 18:38

23. In most manuscripts, the Greek words for the English expression "for this" are repeated twice in the passage where Jesus talks about his mission to bear witness for the truth, just like in the English quote cited above. It seems that the person who copied this particular codex might have chosen to write these two words only once, maybe due to lack of space. This does not change the contents of the text; it just makes the language a little less formal.

Testament today, are these the same as the originals? Or is it reasonable to suspect that the contents for one reason or the other have been changed over time?"

"This is perhaps the most important insight from this particular fragment," smiled Alex. "Some scholars used to believe that the gospel of John might have been distorted over the years, as this gospel differs so much from the other three. But this fragment—perhaps copied directly from the original—is a telling proof that the texts we have today are more or less exactly the same as the original."

Sherlock became deeply absorbed in thought. "This is incredibly relevant information to our case . . . " he said, got up from his chair and started to button his long coat. "I think our business here is complete. Homeward?"

†

Not much was said when the company took their seats on the train back home. Halfway back to London, though, Sherlock was struck by an urgent thought: "By the way, Dr Barkley . . . sorry—Alex. There's a somewhat important detail that we haven't really touched upon so far during our investigation. Until now, we've taken for granted the premise that Jesus of Nazareth is a real, historical person. Could you as a scholar finally confirm this before we go our separate ways tonight?"

Alex Barkley gave a warm smile and nodded: "An excellent question. Luckily enough, there's also an indisputable answer. On one hand, Jesus of Nazareth lived his life in a rather remote corner of the Roman Empire. He had no political ambitions, he didn't write anything himself, and he was only active in public for maybe three years before he was executed. On the other hand, he's still one of the most extensively documented persons in antiquity."

"Though I assume that the gospels are the only sources to his life?" wondered John.

"By no means," replied Alex. "There are both Jewish and Roman historians that mention Jesus. But these are of course much weaker as historical sources. They don't have the same contact with eyewitnesses, and they're more remote in time and space. But let's do a thought experiment," he suggested. "Let's throw away every copy of the gospels. Yes, let's go even further and also get rid of all other early Christian sources. In that case, we would still know the following:" Alex put his hand on the table between them and enumerated each point on his fingers.

"Jesus of Nazareth was a Jewish teacher who was known to heal people and cast out evil spirits. Several people thought that he was the Messiah. However, he was rejected by the Jewish leaders, and was executed by crucifixion in Jerusalem under Pontius Pilate, during the time that Tiberius was emperor in Rome. Despite his shameful death, the message that Jesus was risen from the dead spread fast over the Roman empire, to such an extent that all kinds of people, from cities and countryside, men and women, free people and slaves worshipped him as God, and as early as 64 AD there were large numbers of them as far away as in the metropolis of Rome."[24]

Sherlock murmured: "That was explicit information."

"Furthermore," continued Alex. "If we now should decide to bring back the significantly closer sources that compose the New Testament, Jesus becomes far better documented than almost everyone else during antiquity, both when it comes to eyewitness reports and number of early documents. I haven't heard anyone question the existence of Pericles in Athens, or Spartacus or Brutus in Rome. Still, the source material about their lives and activities is considerably weaker." Alex leaned back in his seat as if to give a physical demonstration of his comfortable scholarly position.

"We may therefore securely lean back in the knowledge that Jesus of Nazareth was a real historical person, who despite his insignificant work field has had a larger impact on human history than any of the Roman emperors with all their power."

The train approached Watford Station and started to slow down. Alex rose and got ready to get off, in order to get home to Hertford. But there was one more point he had to make before he took his leave. He decided to get straight to the point: "So I guess I'll see you in church next time?"

"Pardon?" Sherlock looked up in surprise.

"Well, the thing is . . . " Alex Barkley became slightly insecure, looked down on the floor and said: "It was actually I who came to you to get some help with a case, not the opposite . . . "

Sherlock looked somewhat embarrassed. "Dear me, I completely forgot that you too had a case to solve!" He quickly regained his composure. "I'll obviously do all I can to restore your lost cross. Obviously, I need access to the crime scene and a chance to interview some key persons."

The train stopped with a jerk. Alex didn't want to miss his stop, and needed a quick decision:

---

24. Alex' account here resembles the one given by history professor Edwin Yamauchi, interviewed in Strobel, Lee *The case for Christ* (Zondervan 1998) p 114

"Alright then, come to the service Sunday morning. That would be the easiest time to meet all of the people concerned. For now, I'll return to my temporary nest. Thank you for your willingness to come along on this unplanned trip."

"The pleasure was entirely ours," John replied enthusiastically, got up and shook the hand of their historical guide. Sherlock followed his example: "Yes. It's been a long time since a visit to Manchester was so rewarding."

CHAPTER 9

SUNDAY EXCURSION

THE FOLLOWING SUNDAY, a few minutes before the morning service, Sherlock Holmes and John H Watson were gathered by the entrance to the old stone church in Hertford. Sherlock kept tramping around impatiently on the gravel outside the church, while people passed them on their way inside. A churchwarden soon came out and shook their hands:

"Mr Holmes and Dr Watson, I presume? Reverend Barkley told me you were coming. Please step inside!"

Sherlock gave him a reserved nod, and with John at his heels, he walked into the church. Once inside, he discreetly slipped between the last two benches and sat himself down, half-concealed behind a pillar. John thought it fit to follow along. They took off their coats and laid them on the bench beside them. John leaned over to Sherlock and whispered, quite amused: "You're not really behaving like your normal outspoken self today, are you?"

"I don't think I've been at a church service since confirmation," Sherlock hissed back. "I can't keep up with all the stand ups-sit downs and all the say-after-the-priest-exercises. Let's remain here and avoid making a fuss until the whole thing is over."

The church-bells rang, and service began. Today nobody could have failed to guess the occupation of Alex Barkley, dressed as he was in his white priestal robe and with a purple stole hanging over his shoulders. The service proceeded without any unexpected events; John tried to follow the procedure as well as he could, while Sherlock spent his time examining the building and the congregation from his place in the back. The only time he seemed to listen carefully was during the reading of the creed.

He was crucified under Pontius Pilate,

he suffered death and was buried.

On the third day he rose again

John once again leaned over to his friend: "I guess we're fully ready to agree with the 'crucified, dead and buried' part. It's the rest that remains a mystery . . . " he smiled and nudged Sherlock gently in the side. The latter didn't react with either words or body language. John therefore let him be.

When the postlude had died away and the rest of the people had left, Alex came down to the two new visitors. He was now dressed in his regular clerical shirt.

"How nice to see both of you here today!" he greeted them. "Any feedback on the service?"

"Not too long. However, I'm first and foremost here to investigate a theft," replied Sherlock, cutting off their host's attempt at chit-chat. "So, shall we go and examine the scene of the crime?"

"Of course," replied the priest, and quickly assumed a more serious appearance. "Though it would probably be easier to examine the building more thoroughly when the people have gone home when after-church coffee is finished."

"What the . . . " Sherlock checked himself, but couldn't control his irritation entirely. "You serve *coffee* at the scene of the crime? Today?"

"Well . . . yes . . . " Alex' happy mood from just a minute ago had quickly vanished.

Sherlock put his palm across his face in frustration:

"And how did you imagine I'd be able to find any clues to something when people have been trudging about, spilling coffee and dropping biscuit crumbs all over the place? I obviously assumed that the church hall would be sealed and unused until I had the chance to examine the place carefully!"

Their host blushed deeply.

"I'm sorry, I didn't think . . . "

"Yes, that's often the problem when cases remain unsolved," interrupted Sherlock dryly. "Alright then, nothing to do about it now. In the current situation I would still like to talk with some of those who were in the building the night the cross disappeared. But first I'd like to start with your IT technician, the guy who sat two rows in front of us."

"But how . . . ?" began Alex.

"It takes too much time!" said Sherlock deprecatingly. "Shall we just get on with this before everybody sets off home?"

Alex didn't really have anything to add, so he showed his visitors the way out through the church gate. The three men walked quietly outside, traversed the gravelled churchyard, and went over to the church hall across the street.

†

For almost an hour, Sherlock conducted brief conversations with some of the members of the congregation, one at a time. Only the interview with the IT technician at the alarm system by the entrance took slightly longer to perform. In the meantime, John tried his best to excuse his companion's brusque behaviour, though he had the feeling that he didn't succeed entirely.

After having performed these interviews, and after the departure of the last of the congregation, Sherlock spent the next half-hour performing a thorough inspection of the building. It was a church hall of at least two thousand square feet, furnished with tables and chairs, with a piano at one end. The ceiling height was at least three yards, and the windows facing south were also quite tall. On sunny summer days it must get really hot in here, thought John, as he was trying to form an opinion of the building and the possibilities for a burglar to get out an object as large as a two-feet tall cross without being discovered.

Meanwhile, Sherlock was incredibly active in his examination of the place. He started with the table where the cross had been, and continued with an inspection of the floor thereunder. Then he checked all doors of the building, plus the ground outside. Sometimes joyfully humming, sometimes angrily muttering to himself. He even asked Alex to get him a ladder in order to open the roof windows facing north, as well as the trap door to an attic-like chamber at the west gable, plus examining the areas around these. John and Alex never intruded during Sherlock's labour, they only watched quietly.

"Very well then, I wouldn't be surprised if we could be onto something here!" Finally, Sherlock was done. Demonstratively, he dusted off his hands and sat down at one of the tables, where the two other men were already comfortably seated in the low chairs. "With a little bit of luck I think you may have your lost object back again within a few weeks."

Alex Barkley tried to remain calm, but unintentionally jumped a little at these words.

"Well, I don't think I would dare to hope for anything until the cross is actually back here again." His voice sounded calm, though with a slight ray of hope.

"Oh, we'll see, we'll see!" Sherlock said with a secretive smile. "Though I suggest that you keep the alarm on in here. You never know what a potential thief might have in mind."

The detective leaned his head back and closed his eyes. Maybe ten seconds passed by, before he gave a start and regained control of the situation.

"Alright, while we're here together: there's one question that a lot of things seems to hang upon: Are we completely certain that the grave was actually empty?"

The priest racked his brain in an effort to figure out what his guest meant, and what significance his question might have for the lost cross.

"The grave in Jerusalem, that is, not here in Hertford!" interjected Sherlock, before Alex could find the words to respond.

"Oh!" The host for the day quickly changed his mental compass back to antiquity. "Now, do you ask me as a priest or as a scholar?"

"As a scholar, obviously. As I said earlier: in order to solve this riddle, we first need to know the answer to the decisive question: Was the tomb truly empty, or could there be alternative possibilities?"

"This is a pivotal question. We might have to get a snack before we can get through this one." Alex rose and started to walk towards the kitchen. After a few steps he stopped and turned around. "You might as well remain seated, while I find something for us to eat. I would estimate this as a three-sandwich problem."

"Funny guy, that priest," muttered Sherlock.

Chapter 10

TOMB DESERTED

"That hit the spot!" John said contentedly after having finished his first cheddar sandwich.

"Well, one has to go back to fixing one's own meals again . . . " sighed Alex. There was a feeling of listlessness over his person.

"You don't seem to enjoy your new bachelor status very much," commented Sherlock and grabbed his second sandwich.

"It´s a misery." Alex sounded truly bitter. "Sure, I liven up a bit when something interesting turns up here at work, or, well . . . when I happened to get involved in this historical problem of yours. But in the meantime, the loneliness really eats at me. I guess you don't know what you've got till it's gone."

"Talking of deserted places . . . " Sherlock was keen on returning to the track they had just left. "So far, we've established two facts. One: Jesus died. And two: Jesus was buried in a known grave. Could you now—as a scholar—take us one step further and help us establish the status of Jesus' tomb on the morning of the third day after the cross?"

Alex thought for a moment, before he replied: "Let me begin by posing a counter-question: Have you ever heard of any account from the first century, arguing that the tomb was *not* empty?"

John was the first to accept the challenge: "I'm sure that I'm way behind both of you on this subject, though I know I've seen a number of alternative suggestions on what might have happened with Jesus' body after the burial."

"That's correct," Alex confirmed. "There were people, both in Jerusalem and elsewhere who rejected the resurrection and presented competing alternatives concerning the body.[25] My question is a different one, though: Do you know of any early versions that contradict the statement of the empty tomb?" Alex made himself comfortable in his chair, laid one leg over the other with a curious but still secure expression. Both visitors thought intensely while chewing.

"A telling silence, don't you think?" smiled the waiting expert after some time. "And you know what? It was equally silent the decades before, during and after the gospels were written. There simply weren't any accounts around which called the empty tomb in question."

"Just a moment," objected John. "Couldn't it have been the case that there *were* such stories earlier, but that they were destroyed when Christianity took over in the Roman empire?"

"Not a chance," Alex replied immediately. "You have to remember that for three hundred years Christianity was a rebel movement. Three hundred years is a long time—a lot longer than the period from the French Revolution and up till today, to give one example. Moreover, during this period of persecution, huge efforts were made to put an end to the Christian faith, and its devotees were continually tortured and executed for their belief. There were lots of people around who were very critical towards Christianity, and several such writings are preserved from the first centuries. What's interesting to us, though, is the fact that nobody—not a single one of these—state the idea that the tomb should *not* have been empty.[26] And what does this tell us?"

Sherlock just smiled. "You're a good analyst, reverend! You find the angles that might shed some light on this problem. This is absolutely correct: If an adversary appears to have the chance to attack an essential piece of information, but chooses not to do so, it says a lot about the strength of the information."

"I may have to add a saving clause here," John pointed out. "The fact that we don't have any alternative accounts of the contents of the tomb on Sunday morning doesn't mean that we have to accept the gospels at face

25. A summary of competing hypotheses of the time is further explained for instance in Wright, N.T *The Resurrection of the Son of God: Christian Origins and the Question of God* (Fortress Press 2003)

26. Habermas/Licona *The case for the resurrection of Jesus*, p 70

value. We have to keep in mind that they were written by the very same people who intended to spread the message that Jesus was risen."

"An important objection, John. Though not entirely on the spot here," interposed Alex. "There's at least one reason why we shouldn't just reject the gospels out of hand, namely that the Christian movement didn't start spontaneously out of the blue, but in the very city where the events were said to have taken place!"

"That's a good point," supplemented Sherlock. "In my course of work, I often encounter people who present completely fabricated stories. These stories usually have a distinct unifying factor: The storytellers think that nobody will be able to call their bluff."

"I think I follow your line of reasoning," commented Alex. "Are the two of you by any chance familiar with the Mormons?"

Sherlock calmly shook his head, and John raised his eyebrows at this unexpected turn in the conversation. "Vaguely," he replied. "Neat suits, but I can't claim to know their beliefs."

"Well, their teachings aren't of particular importance to us here," continued Alex. "The point I want to make concerns the historical connection. The Book of Mormon claims that a group of Israelites took a couple of boats and sailed over to America, where they experienced a lot of different things."

"What if it isn't the Jesus and Joseph of Arimathea story back again," mumbled Sherlock.

"Something of that kind, maybe. The interesting point to us is that there is no connection between these people and other source material," explained Alex. "The only source to this information is the founder of Mormonism, Joseph Smith, who claimed that he had received some golden plates with secret messages about these events, which only he could understand.[27] Apart from Smith's words there's no historical confirmation whatsoever of these stories. They just had to be taken at face value. And, above all, there was no way to check them, because Smith claimed to have handed the plates back to the angel from whom he'd received them."

---

27. For an external study of the events surrounding these golden plates, see Taves, Ann "History and the Claims of Revelation: Joseph Smith and the Materialization of the Golden Plates" *Numen: International Review for the History of Religions* 61/1–2 Electronic version at http://www.religion.ucsb.edu/wp-content/uploads/B-6-Golden-Plates-Numen.pdf

Sherlock rolled his eyes. "What's wrong with people? Was there no sane person around to sound that Smith guy out and demand to see those golden plates?"

"Oh, yes. A few of his followers claimed to have seen the plates. But most of these still chose to leave the movement some time later." Alex made a pause. "In the case of Jesus, however, all the witnesses held on to the group and their testimony, all the way to their death. That might say something."

John couldn't but agree. He tried to follow the argument to its conclusion: "So your point is that the main difference between Joseph Smith's stories and the situation in Jerusalem is that those who heard the message about the resurrection had direct access to the places and people involved?"

"Exactly!" replied Alex. "It's rather compelling that the Christian movement arose in Jerusalem—the place where Jesus had just been executed and buried! Anyone who was in doubt could go and ask the witnesses and demand to see the tomb themselves."

John thought for a moment. He didn't really have a problem with the line of reasoning. Still, there was a more personal question he wished to ask: "By the way, how do you combine your two roles? I mean, on the one hand performing a critical scrutiny of these texts as a scholar, and on the other hand proclaiming: 'The word of the Lord', like you did in church earlier today."

"I don't really see a contradiction between the two roles," explained Alex. "As a scholar, I treat the gospels just like any other historical documents, and I use the same source criticism I would use with other ancient texts. These studies increase my conviction that the gospels are reliable as historical documents. While as a priest and . . . well, also a personal believer, I derive tremendous joy from the gospels. As you might know, the word "gospel" means "joyful message." Therefore, I think that these texts are not only historically reliable, but that God also speaks to us through them."

"So, what problems does the critical scholar Dr Barkley see with the reports of the empty tomb?" asked Sherlock, leaning eagerly forward in his chair.

"This is actually one of the most intriguing details in the four accounts," smiled Alex. "Although perhaps not in the way we might think at first glance. Let's create a parallel example: Imagine that we want to spread a rumour of something really incredible."

"A man with two heads!" cried John with a spontaneous smile.

"Alright then," chuckled Alex. "Now, if we wanted to spread the story of this two-headed man over the world, on what would we build such a story? Remember that there were no cameras during antiquity, so we have to rely on personal testimonies."

"I'd imagine that we need witnesses with extremely high credibility, in order to succeed with such a task," laughed John.

"I would think so," Alex replied. "Now, the proposal that a dead man has returned to life does indeed seem at least as incredible as a man with two heads. And here's the key question: Are there any really reliable witnesses to the empty tomb?"

"I've studied the four accounts of these events as closely as possible," said Sherlock. "They're really quite different from each other. But there are some pieces of information that occur in all four of them."

"Precisely what I wanted to point out," exclaimed Alex Barkley. "You two have worked with many crime investigations together. What conclusion do you make of the fact that the discovery of the empty tomb is described so differently in the four gospels?"

"I find it very hard to get a coherent picture," began John. "On the train this morning I took some time to read through the four accounts. And they really differ in their details. The authors name different numbers of women. Were there any guards of not? What happened with the stone covering the opening? You get different information of how many angels they meet. The women act differently after leaving the tomb—and so on. Doesn't this create a huge obstacle for the credibility?" John turned to his friend for support.

Sherlock rubbed his hands in glee. "Do you remember the traffic accident you were involved in last autumn, John?"

John twitched slightly at the change of subject: "Of course—that was the day my old car became scrap. Luckily, nobody was injured."

"Yes, but you remember how many people who had to file their reports of the accident?"

"Well, that's what the insurance company required . . . "

"Now, do you remember how different these reports were? Some mentioned differing details about the cars, some described how the drivers acted, and others emphasized the traffic rules and which direction the cars came from. The stories were quite different, but there was at least one piece of information that was clear as crystal."

"That it wasn't my fault!"

Sherlock smiled towards his flatmate. "Well, everybody didn't agree on that point. Still, there's at least one thing we actually know: There were two cars that collided, and you were involved. And—if we were to be completely impartial—it would be worse if the witnesses gave exactly the same descriptions of what had happened, as it would indicate the witnesses having made up a story together."

Sherlock left the analogy and returned to the issue at stake: "Differing accounts of an event, however, indicates independent sources. These kinds of sources are also very valuable in an inquiry such as this. In the same way the gospels share at least one common piece of information concerning the events after Jesus' burial: On the morning of the third day after the crucifixion, a group of women came to the tomb, and found it empty."

"That's correct," filled Alex in. "And this is the crux of the matter. The fact that the four accounts show differences in other details doesn't ruin their credibility in the main question—rather the opposite."

"Nevertheless, there is still one important remaining question," added John. "Even if we have independent witness reports—do they actually tell the truth? I mean . . . angels, dead men walking . . . "

"Let's take one thing at a time," interrupted Alex. "Our current focus is a very natural one: Was the tomb empty or not? If we return to the witnesses mentioned, they were all women, which was a huge problem at the time. In this culture women were considered to be the weaker sex, not just physically, but across the whole field. They weren't thought of as reliable people. In a normal trial, women were not trusted as witnesses."[28]

"Sounds a bit sexist?" John muttered sardonically.

"Yes, well . . . " continued Alex, oblivious to John's sarcastic tone. "But that was the culture back then. We can just picture the disciples' reactions when the women return from the grave and tell them they had met an angel who told them that Jesus was risen." Alex once again took out his mobile to check the Bible quote. "Here it is; Luke writes: 'But they did not believe the women, because their words seemed to them like nonsense.'"[29]

"Seems like a very reasonable reaction in the situation," John interjected.

28. Josephus is one of those who underline the weak role of female witnesses, in a passage where he lays out general rules for witnesses in trials: "But let not the testimony of women be admitted, on account of the levity and boldness of their sex" Josephus, *Antiquities of the Jews*, 4.8.15

29. Luke 24:11

"We may also mention Celsus," Alex continued. "He was a Greek philosopher in the second century, who passionately wanted to eradicate Christianity. He explained that the resurrection could not possibly be true, as it depended on witness reports from women, as everybody knows that you can't trust the words of hysterical women."[30]

"Absurd!" exclaimed John.

"Still, you have to remember that in Celsus' time, it was a severe blow to an account if you could show that it was based on a woman's statement, instead of a man's. Let's now imagine someone wanting to spread a false rumour that Jesus' corpse had suddenly disappeared from the tomb. What witnesses would they have chosen in order to appear as credible as possible? Men with a good reputation, or "hysterical" women?"

The room fell quiet. Alex leaned back comfortably in his chair. He had made his point. Sherlock had remained silent for some time; he wasn't really accustomed to someone else holding the baton during the exposition of a case. Finally, though, he found it fit to wrap things up: "Well, I think we have answered the questions for today. What's your opinion, John?"

His friend nodded. "I guess so. There doesn't seem to be any more stones to turn right now, if you'll allow the expression . . . "

"Then I think we're done for now." Sherlock got up and put on his outer garments. "I think we've reached the point where we can firmly establish the very fact we started out with: the empty tomb. Now we have to think over our next step, in order to proceed."

The three men followed each other to the door. As they descended the steps outside, Sherlock turned abruptly to his host and said: "Lend me your mobile, Alex. There is a word of scripture from the sermon I would like to check."

In glad astonishment, the priest once again opened his Bible app and handed over his mobile. Sherlock responded with a short smile and moved away a few steps. John watched him thoughtfully. There was something in Sherlock's behaviour that seemed familiar. After a minute or so he handed the mobile back with a friendly nod. "Thank you. Very interesting. John, would you care to call for a cab?"

Sherlock turned his heel and walked off. The gravel crunched under his feet as he, with firm steps, walked away towards the road.

---

30. Celsus writes: "But who saw this? A hysterical female, as you say, and perhaps some other one of those who were deluded by the same sorcery." Quoted in Bauckham, Richard *The Women at the Tomb: The Credibility of their Story* http://richardbauckham. co.uk/uploads/Accessible/The%20Women%20&%20the%20Resurrection.pdf

CHAPTER 11

ON THE ROAD

A COUPLE OF DAYS passed. John's days were filled with the mundane and with planning for the future. Sherlock, on the other hand, seemed to have transformed into a bookworm. Whole days passed by without John seeing his flatmate. When he finally did get home, it was often with another thick volume on ancient history under his arm.

Whether or not he made any progress in the case with the lost cross, John never got to know. Neither did he ask. By the time action was needed, Sherlock typically updated him pretty quickly. Before this happened, there was seldom any use in asking.

During the last few days John had been out a couple of times, looking at some used cars. He still hadn't found exactly what he was searching for, but need for a car definitely increased. Not only for personal use, but also to be able to accept medical employment where he had to be more mobile.

One Thursday afternoon in the transition between March and April, he took the stairs down from the flat, planning to take the underground to Holborn to look at a small Toyota which he had found on the web. On the way out John bumped into Mrs Hudson, who came through the front door with some small shopping bags in her hand.

"Dear me, Dr Watson!" she exclaimed with a small giggle, after having almost collided with her tenant in the doorway. "I haven't seen the two of you in a while. What have you been up to lately?"

"Would you believe me if I told you that Sherlock seems stuck with his strangest case so far?" John replied.

"Sounds quite normal to me," she said. "I haven't seen any dodgy-looking men or heard any nocturnal racket from your rooms lately, though. Might he possibly start to adjust himself to more normal working hours?" she asked in a slightly hopeful voice.

John answered calmly: "There's only one thing I've learnt to be sure of when it comes to Sherlock Holmes. And that is never to be sure of anything at all."

"Well then, as long as nobody gets hurt and the walls keep standing, I wish you the best of luck in . . . well, whatever it is you're up to."

"Hopefully the result of this day's business will be that I acquire a car," replied John, with a friendly pat on Mrs Hudson's shoulder. "In that case I could take you on a Sunday morning drive some day!"

"Sounds lovely," she smiled back, but added tentatively. "I hope this doesn't mean you're leaving Baker Street, though! I understand it's really hard to find a good parking in this part of town."

"I can assure you that I have no intention of leaving, Mrs Hudson," he smiled and bade his landlady farewell. He made the short walk down to the underground, which took him the few stations over to the small inner-city street where he had agreed to meet the man who might have just the car he was looking for.

This time the encounter actually turned out the way John had hoped. The small Toyota went smoothly during the test drive. Despite being eight years old, both the engine and body looked fine. The paperwork was in order, and John also managed to negotiate the price down to the level he had planned. Registration papers and money transfer were taken care of on the spot, and moments later John Watson stood on the pavement, eyeing his new vehicle. At this very moment a familiar character turned the corner.

"Sherlock!" exclaimed John in surprise. "Come on, have you been stalking me to check what car I was going to buy?"

Sherlock came up to his flatmate and smiled indulgently. "I'm sure I would be told sooner or later if you were to actually purchase a vehicle." He laid his hand on the bonnet. "Are you keen on this one?"

John triumphantly held up his key. "Just bought it!"

Sherlock nodded, put his hands on his back and strolled curiously around the car.

"What about you, then? What have you been up to if you've devoted yourself to other business than spying on me?" wondered John.

"The British Museum!" Sherlock stopped and looked up from the car. "Did you know they have the world's largest collection of Egyptian mummies outside Cairo? It's incredibly interesting to study how they wrapped and embalmed their dead."

John couldn't help smiling at the excursion. "You seem to have a pretty strong interest in death right now."

"It sort of goes with my occupation," retorted Sherlock coldly. "Still, this is obviously the first time I take this much time to investigate ancient deaths."

John opened the driver's door. "Well, I'll be driving home, and can hopefully also find a parking spot nearby our place. Like to come along?"

"How could I miss a maiden tour!" replied Sherlock in a jolly mood, opened the passenger door and looked inside with curiosity, and then made himself comfortable in his seat.

John sat down, turned the key, and the car gently rolled away.

"Did you hear how nicely the ignition started?" he exclaimed and carefully stroked the steering wheel. "Let's hope that it'll work this well in the future too. I don't really have your gifts, so I don't know that much about the seller and his skills at taking care of a car," smiled John.

Sherlock looked out the side window, impatiently tapping with his fingers on the dashboard. Finally he couldn't keep silent any more:

"OK—shall we deal with it now, or do you want to wait and see how things go?"

John took a firmer grip around the wheel and his face turned dogged.

"You know, there are still some limitations to your abilities. This time I have an advantage you can't compete with. I've met the guy, that's more than you have."

"A car is a remarkable thing," replied Sherlock calmly. "No matter how well the owner wants to cover his tracks, a car still tells a story about its driver."

Almost absent-mindedly, Sherlock pulled down the sunshade above him and took a close look. "Aha, I thought as much," he mumbled and leaned comfortably back in his seat.

For a few seconds, John went through an inner struggle, but he soon realized that there probably was no way back. He braked by a traffic light and sighed: "Alright—give it to me. What kind of person is he?"

"Well, I've only had time for a quick glance. It seems obvious, though, that this is a rather careless and impatient gentleman. He's single, lives in town and parties quite a bit, even though his economy isn't that good. This may perhaps be explained by the fact that he switches girlfriends every now and then. And finally he smokes—Camel." Sherlock fell silent for a second. "I'm not sure I would buy a used car from a man like that. But then again, the car might obviously work out anyway."

The lights went green. John jerked at the gearstick and the Toyota emitted a grinding noise as he failed to slip it properly into first gear. The car behind them honked angrily. Finally, John found the gear and managed to get away. He stared decisively on the road ahead, but said nothing.

"You probably must have discovered the impatient personality yourself, at least when you checked the wheels," continued Sherlock calmly. John still remained quiet.

"The tires are new, but the tread is still heavily torn. This indicates that he accelerates and brakes violently by turns. This is also confirmed if you look at the trip computer here," pointed the detective. "He hasn't cared to reset the petrol consumption. Now, you don't get an average consumption this high with a normal driving style in the city, let alone with longer driving distances. So there can be little doubt that we're dealing with an inner-city man with a short temper."

"But the smoking?" objected John. "I can't smell any tobacco!"

"No, he's used one of these deodorants that car dealers use specifically to conceal smoke odour. And if you look closely here between the front seats, you see a number of small marks in the plastic at about the same place."

Sherlock pointed at the spot, and with some effort he went on to pull out the cigarette lighter and held it diagonally against the marks. "The lighter is a bit stuck, but as you can see, it fits exactly with these marks if you sit in the driver's seat and occasionally hit the lighter against this place. It seems as he's frequently become irritated, perhaps by the difficulty of getting the lighter out. Now, he has actually cleaned the ashtray inside, but on the outside you can find small traces of ashes from Camel cigarettes," concluded Sherlock.

John remembered Sherlock having performed an in-depth study of different types of tobacco ashes. This seemed to be a case when this knowledge actually seemed to be of some use, John figured. He continued through the slow rush hour traffic, still without taking his eyes off the road.

"And how do you explain the partying and the girlfriends?"

"To begin with, he's an obvious single. The car mat on your side is heavily torn, but the backseat and the carpets there are virtually unused. The mat here under me is also in pretty good condition, although there are some marks that can hardly come from anything but high-heeled shoes. They're also heels of many different shapes, I might add. This indicates either a woman who changes shoes very often, or a man who changes women frequently. I'd put my money on the latter. When I went on to check the sunshade here, he hasn't bothered to clean this either. Here's plenty of fingerprints with powder and also some lipstick. Different types of powder, and some colourful lipsticks. All of this gives the picture of a man who picks up different women who do their make-up in the car, while they drive away for a club night."

John sighed again. "Ok. And finally: the economy?"

"Well, what's your opinion—would a man with this kind of lifestyle drive a Toyota if he could afford a sports car?"

Hard to believe that the satisfaction over a new car could dissipate so dramatically in just five minutes, thought John, in morose silence.

"Still, this vehicle might of course be great for you anyway," said Sherlock in an attempt to melt some of the icy atmosphere. The driver made no reply.

The car turned left into Euston Road. In this heavy traffic it would probably take another fifteen minutes to get to the northern end of Baker Street. John decided to swallow his irritation and return to their ongoing case.

"So you've been looking at mummies at the museum today?" he began in a restrained voice. "I find it slightly difficult to see how this could give us more information on what happened to Jesus' body after the burial."

"Well, almost all mummies predate Christianity, so they aren't exact parallels, "explained Sherlock, apparently glad to find a new subject of conversation. "The Egyptians and the Jews also had different methods of taking care of their dead. Though when it comes to wrapping the bodies, there are some similarities. By the way, do you remember the seemingly irrelevant detail that the apostle John gives about the linen strips in the tomb?"

John shook his head, meanwhile concentrating upon the traffic. "Sorry, I must have considered it too unimportant to make a mental note of."

"John occasionally mentions this kind of minor detail that seems to be of no importance to the rest of the account," Sherlock added. "When this happens in a story, it's something noteworthy."

"Because it indicates that the author's making things up?"

"On the contrary, John." Sherlock turned towards the driver. "Listen carefully now, this is classic interrogation technique. A useful method to separate an authentic witness report from a false one is when the witness mentions these kinds of small details that you usually wouldn't include in a fake story. Such details just complicate things for the investigator, and a liar normally wants to deliver a straight and clear account that doesn't raise any questions."

John started to get impatient, and wanted to cut to the chase.

"So what's your point concerning the linen strips?"

"Here's the deal: First John gives these minor details about how fast he and Peter run to the grave, how they behave at the grave entrance, and so on.[31] But then John writes that Peter went inside the tomb and saw the linen strips. And then he adds this seemingly unimportant detail, that there was also some kind of head cloth, which they found rolled up in a place by itself."[32]

Sherlock paused. "Now, do you draw any particular conclusion from this detail, if we for the moment should assume it as correct?"

John laughed and shook his head. "You're the detective here. As a doctor I just feel a bit uneasy over the handling of a deceased man, that somebody would have put such great effort into unwrapping the burial shroud from a man that had been dead for little more than twenty-four hours, and then leave it neatly behind in the tomb. I mean, why? If someone wanted to steal the body, why not just grab it and then clear off as fast as possible? Why take the trouble of both desecrating the corpse, as well as running the risk of being discovered?"

Sherlock's smile grew wider across his face.

"Very good, John—very good! This is exactly the type of questions an interrogator would ask. *Where is the motive?* Without intent there would be no frauds—ever. As long as no motive appears, we must remain hesitant towards the grave robber hypothesis."

John turned into Baker Street and started looking for a parking space. However much he searched, though, no available space would appear. A sense of frustration came over him.

---

31. The text does not explicitly mention John's name, but most scholars agree that the phrase "the disciple whom Jesus loved" refers to John himself.

32. John 21:7

"You know . . . Sometimes I get the idea that some problems just don't have a solution. What if the case of the empty tomb is such a problem? Maybe we just have to drop it?"

Sherlock once again turned straight towards his driver and answered with a firm tone: "John, haven't I reminded you a thousand times about the most important rule every detective, every investigator, every seeker of truth has to abide by? Once we've got all facts on the table, we must honestly and without mercy try every possible explanation. When we have excluded all alternatives that are either unthinkable or practically impossible, and only one alternative remains, this implacably has to be the truth."

John had trouble concentrating upon Sherlock's words; he was too busy looking for a parking space. Finally, he gave up.

"Alright, here's what we'll do," he suggested. "I let you off outside our front door, and then I'll drive around till I find some parking."

Sherlock quickly got out of the car, and the two men went their separate ways, each one continuing his own search.

CHAPTER 12

A CASE OF CORRUPTION

MORE THAN AN HOUR passed before John showed up back home. He could see the coloured light from the TV across the furniture in the living room.

"I didn't know it was this difficult to park in central London!" he called out. "Finally, I had to hire a spot in a garage up at Sussex Place and pay for a fortnight."

No answer was heard from Sherlock, who had stretched himself out in front of the TV. No interest in chit-chat there, apparently, thought John and went into the kitchen to find an evening snack. He discovered half a pizza in the fridge.

"You wouldn't consider it a serious crime if I grab this pizza?" he said loudly to the detective, who was watching the news without paying too much attention.

"Feel free!" came the answer from the living room.

John put the pizza half in the microwave and turned it on.

"By the way, I've been thinking a bit more about Jesus' corpse," called John towards the living room. "I mean, how fast does a dead body decay in the heat of the Middle East?"

"Would you want the figure in number of days, or in percentage of decomposition?"

The answer came without delay from just behind John's back. He started, and turned quickly around. Sherlock stood comfortably leaning against the doorpost, smiling, his arms folded.

"Come on then," continued the detective. "Interested or not?"

"The news wasn't that interesting anymore?" countered John.

"Domestic politics. Always the same, incredibly humdrum. Deaths are always more exciting." Sherlock sat up on the kitchen worktop. "So, a penny for your thoughts!"

John took the pizza out of the microwave and sat down at the small kitchen table beside.

"Well, here's my point: If we accept the traditional chronology, some 50 days had passed after the crucifixion before Peter and the others started to preach the resurrection publicly. Isn't it plausible that a body could decompose rather quickly in the hot climate of the Middle-East? In that case people might just have been mistaken, even if they did go to the grave to find not much more than a skeleton?"

"Impossible," replied Sherlock without an ounce of hesitation.

"But . . . why?"

"Not by medical reasons, obviously. The rate of decomposition for a human body is an incredibly interesting subject." Sherlock began to get that particular glow of enthusiasm. "I've studied . . . "

John quickly interrupted: "No thanks. Not interested in any details. At least not while I'm eating."

Sherlock gave a short laugh: "Alright. You see, the problem lies more on a psychological level." He sat down opposite his eating companion. "Let's make a thought experiment. We presume that I die. Right out of the blue."

"Wow—that's drastic!"

"Yep!" Sherlock didn't appear to find anything troubling with the example. "I get buried—weeping and gnashing of teeth, thanks and goodbye. After that, we could imagine a long time span, let's say a whole year. Then a rumour suddenly arises: *Sherlock Holmes has been seen in the alleys at night. He's alive!* Quite naturally, you get confused, and therefore decide to run off and dig up my grave to reopen my coffin. And then you'd find . . . what?"

"Then I'd most probably find myself arrested for disturbance of a grave . . . " John smiled, finding it hard to take the example very seriously. Nevertheless, he decided to follow the trail for the sake of the discussion: "Seriously speaking, it seems obvious that I would in that case find a corpse that had progressed quite far in the process of corruption. It wouldn't make pleasant viewing at all."

"Hardly recommendable," agreed Sherlock. "Now, let's presume that my body would be destroyed beyond any recognition. Nobody would have been able to tell at first sight that the contents in the coffin ever had been me! In that case, wouldn't you have reached the conclusion that the rumours were true and that I'd risen again?"

John laughed, got up and started to put the dishes into the dishwasher.

"What do you think of me? No person is that easily fooled. Anyone would understand that a corpse becomes more and more unrecognizable each day that passes by."

Hardly had he finished the sentence, when he saw the full significance of this insight for the case of the empty tomb. He turned around and looked straight at Sherlock.

"You mean that as long as *any* human remains were discovered in the tomb, no one would have drawn the conclusion that Jesus was risen?"

"Obviously!" Sherlock got up from his chair and accompanied John into the living-room. The two men sat down opposite each other by the coffee-table. The detective continued his train of thought: "One thing that I've noted during the last couple of weeks is that there are quite a few present-day pundits who seem to presuppose that people during antiquity were morons. A rather rash conclusion, if you ask me. No sane person—then or now—would believe that a dead man suddenly becomes alive again, unless they're presented with extraordinary evidence."

John nodded thoughtfully, while Sherlock went on: "Nevertheless, there was a rapidly growing movement which arose in Jerusalem, emphatically arguing that Jesus' body wasn't merely gone, but that he'd actually risen again from the dead. Such a movement would have been completely impossible as long as *some* kind of human remains still remained in the tomb."

John thought intensely. "Can't we suppose some kind of conspiracy?" John now took the opportunity to put forward a number of odd hypotheses that he'd managed to come up with. "That this Joseph of Arimathea made a secret pact with Pilate, or maybe that . . . "

Sherlock just shook his head with a tired look. "Sure, and the CIA planned the 9/11 attacks . . . " he replied in a sour tone.

"I've obviously evaluated these loose ends too. But they all lead to dead ends. You know, John . . . "

Sherlock sighed. "After a while in a business such as mine, you get quite sick of all these dogmatists who constantly want to patch together explanations of their own, concocted back at their own chambers. And it's always those people who don't have a real clue about the actual circumstances. The larger the case, the larger the chance that someone puts forward this type of wild speculation."

He made a rhetorical pause. "However, there's one common feature in these explanations."

"And that is . . . ?"

"A complete lack of historical evidence," replied Sherlock abruptly. "You see, I've spent a few weeks studying this particular case, and I can easily name at least twenty more or less sweeping suggestions of what *might have* happened . . . I'm sorry, I can't put up with this kind of people." Sherlock hid his face on his hands, but soon adjusted himself in the armchair, and regained his professional attitude.

"Listen now, my friend, and let me give you a very simple rule of conduct, which may save both you and others a lot of trouble." Sherlock spoke calmly, and put emphasis on each word:

"Always-start-with-facts!"

John nodded and let the message sink in.

"It may sound like an all too obvious rule, but I'll be damned if it isn't broken all the time." Sherlock sounded genuinely upset. "It's an unbelievable waste of time and energy to start concocting hypotheses, and then proceed to try to squeeze these together with facts. If you follow this working order, you'll sooner or later have to start battering facts to suit your theories, instead of the other way round. But if we uncompromisingly decide to begin a case by gathering all accessible facts, we may go from there and then find our way towards a reliable explanation."

"Surely, this was the way they had been working in this case," John thought to himself. First, they had to establish that Jesus was really dead. Thereafter came the insight that he was buried in a known tomb. And thereafter the crucial point—that the tomb a couple of days later was discovered empty.

"Alright, here we stand with a dead body, laid in a tomb and then completely lost?"

"Exactly—and now we face the really intriguing mystery," Sherlock smiled genially, his eyes sparkling like a child at Christmas. "The mystery of the empty tomb. Somewhere there is a solution. There *has* to be a solution."

"So, which hypotheses do we have to choose from?" John leaned back expectantly, waiting to get the whole picture laid out before him. Now he really began to get into this case. Yet Sherlock abruptly interrupted his thoughts.

"For God's sake, John! Didn't I tell you just seconds ago that we won't get anywhere with wild speculations?" Sherlock resolutely beat his fist against the coffee-table to emphasize his point. "We simply *have* to begin with the task of finding out what more hard facts we can gather, and from these we may then build a solid explanation of what actually might have happened."

At this moment Sherlock's mobile rang. He took it out and checked.

"Why if it isn't our friend the priest!"

The detective pressed the loud-speaker button.

"Good evening, reverend Barkley! We're just sitting here at home, finally settling the matter of the empty tomb."

"Hi there, John speaking!" the doctor said aloud, to indicate that he was listening too.

"Good evening, both of you. That's good news, as the empty tomb is a very well-supported historical fact. I don't know if you've discovered this yet, but a clear majority of scholars who *don't* believe in the resurrection accept the fact that the tomb was empty."[33]

"An interesting piece of information," commented Sherlock. "Let's for the time being consider this point as established."

"I agree completely," the voice came from the phone. "Although ... this wasn't really the purpose of my call. Three days from now, we have a meeting with the church council, and I'm sure they'll be asking me some pointed questions about the chances of getting our cross back. Still, I haven't heard anything from you since we met out here last time."

The phone became quiet. John felt that the atmosphere had suddenly become awkward. They had received some very helpful academic support in their own case, but Sherlock hadn't seemed to take the priest's problem too seriously. John felt deeply ashamed on behalf of his companion.

"Everything is under control, no need for worrying," replied Sherlock coldly. "I'm quite convinced that the cross will be back in its proper place in no more than a week from now."

John looked indignantly at the man opposite him, and mimed soundlessly but clearly: *You haven't done a damn thing! What are you thinking?*

---

33. Gary Habermas, one of the world's leading experts on this subject, has made a compilation of the writings of leading scholars, showing that a clear majority—even when those who deny the resurrection are included—still accept that the tomb was empty, for one reason or another. See Habermas, Gary "Resurrection Research from 1975 to the Present: What are Critical Scholars Saying?" *Journal for the Study of the Historical Jesus,* 3.2 (2005). Electronic version: http://www.garyhabermas.com/articles/J_Study_Historical_Jesus_3-2_2005/J_Study_Historical_Jesus_3-2_2005.htm

Sherlock showed no sign of alarm, but just smiled. The voice from the phone returned, though slightly hesitant.

"Well . . . I'd really like to hope so. Really."

John tried to play down the embarrassing situation. He cleared his throat. "I have to say that it's still very rewarding to talk to you about these Biblical matters, Alex," he said divertingly. "You always give straightforward answers." He hesitated a moment, wondering whether to continue this train of thought, but decided to carry on: "You know, I've heard a number of, should we say . . . wishy-washy people who claim that it doesn't really matter if Jesus was resurrected or not. We can still spread his message of brotherly feeling and so on."

"Pure nonsense!" sniffed Sherlock loudly.

"I'd agree. Well, possibly in somewhat more diplomatic terms . . . " commented Alex over the phone line. "You know, the whole Christian faith stands and falls with the resurrection. If Jesus never rose from the dead, my life has missed the mark."

The phone went silent for a second again. Then the voice returned, now with more confidence: "Actually, the best and earliest source to the resurrection puts it just about that way. Though, as you well know, this text isn't from the gospels, but from a completely different source."

Sherlock suddenly froze. "Pardon me?"

The voice over the phone came back almost immediately.

"My, my . . . I suddenly see that I have other business to attend to. Gentlemen, I wish you a good evening!"

A click came from the phone. The two men in the flat looked at each other in astonishment.

"What did he mean?" wondered John, half to himself. Sherlock remained silent, seemingly quite puzzled. John went on: "Does he possess some kind of still unknown document that he's bought from some Egyptian antique dealer?" John remembered having seen a TV documentary about such affairs. Judging from that documentary, the whole business seemed rather shady. It should really be beneath any serious scholar to deal with those things, thought John to himself.

Sherlock's phone suddenly buzzed. John quickly leaned over the table to see.

> <You get explanation when I get cross. Suggestion: day after tomorrow. Midday Baker St.>

Sherlock gave a loud laugh: "He's throwing down the gauntlet! Alright with me!" The detective looked at his watch. "Well then, time flies. It looks as if tomorrow will be a busy day. Goodnight."

He got up and hurried towards his bedroom door.

"Aren't you going to reply?" called John in vain. With another rumbling laugh Sherlock retreated to his own room, and the door was once again shut between them.

CHAPTER 13

THE KEY IN A LETTER

THE FOLLOWING AFTERNOON, JOHN went over the floor of 221B with the Hoover. As usual, he left Sherlock's bedroom as it was. He did take the liberty, though, of peeking inside through the half-open door. At the detective's bedside table, he could see several thick books, most probably dealing with their historical problem. John turned his eyes back out into the living-room, where Sherlock's old confirmation Bible lay open on the coffee-table.

John smiled to himself. The last couple of weeks had surely meant a remarkable reorientation, not only in topics of discussion, but also when it came to furnishing. Sherlock's collection of chemistry equipment was now stuffed away in a corner, and the heaps of crime literature that normally lay about here and there in the flat were also for the moment heaped up beside the sofa.

The next second, Sherlock came rushing inside with a paper bag under his arm.

"Groceries?" wondered John and put away the vacuum cleaner in its cupboard.

"Man shall not live by bread alone!" Sherlock smiled brightly, apparently very satisfied with the biblical allusion. He unpacked the bag and spread out the day's harvest of academic literature on the coffee-table. "London Library remains a goldmine! Long ago I acquired a membership for life. The peace and quiet is immensely better there than in the bustle and noise at the public libraries."

He grumbled a bit, though not without appreciation: "Our priestly friend thinks he's one step ahead. He ought to think twice before he took up a battle with the world's only consulting detective!"

"So, what have you found?" asked John calmly and sat down in the armchair.

"It's not the gospels that hold the key—it's Paul!" Sherlock glowed with enthusiasm. John felt safer keeping to his sitting on the fence-attitude.

"Paul? Hang on a moment now—he was one of the first Christians' worst opponents. I've understood that it's quite unlikely that he even met Jesus during his short active period."

Sherlock waved deprecatingly. "Look here, I'll show you." He shoved the Bible over to John. "Look up Paul's first letter to the Corinthians, chapter 15."

"You don't want to see yourself?" John looked cautiously up at his flatmate.

"Don't worry, I've been studying the passage half the day; I know it by heart," chuckled Sherlock, but soon went back to a more serious tone of voice: "I think this may possibly be the most important material in the whole case."

John had turned to the correct page. "Alright, the headline says: 'Christ's Resurrection'. Now, tell me why this should be equally important as the gospels?"

"More important, John—more important!" John felt an impulse to take the role as the devil's advocate, though something in Sherlock's commitment made him restrain the impulse. He recognized his companion's emotions, and knew by experience that when Sherlock Holmes had reached this level of enthusiasm, there was nothing that could stop him. John Watson resigned and leaned back with the Bible in his lap.

"OK then—tell me why."

Sherlock calmly sat himself down in the sofa across the table and began his explanation: "As an investigator, it's of the utmost importance to get access to testimonies as close to the event as possible." He made a pause for effect: "This is as close as it gets."

John's eyebrows wrinkled a bit. "Wasn't that what we saw in Manchester?"

"Yup. At least as long as we're talking about the oldest *physical* copy. And if I was being a bit picky, I would state it didn't deal exactly with the event before us. The key to a case like this is to get access to the source that's closest in time after the cross."

"I don't get it," replied John in honest curiosity.

"To begin with," began Sherlock. "This text is beyond doubt written by Paul himself. There is a scholarly discussion about some of the letters that bear Paul's name. This particular letter is however one of those that the whole academic world declares to be a genuine Pauline letter."

"So far I'm with you. But isn't it still quite unlikely that Paul was personally present at these events?"

"Quite probable, but that's not really the crucial point here," countered Sherlock, and pointed with his finger in the Bible. "Look here what he writes: 'I passed on to you as of first importance what I also received'. From there he begins his survey of those who were reported to have been witnesses to the resurrection."[34]

John took over the reading: "Alright, let's see what he passed on. ' . . . That Jesus died for our sins according to the scriptures, and that he was buried,'" John interrupted himself with a smile. "Ok, we've agreed on the 'died and buried' part."

"Do carry on," Sherlock replied calmly.

"' . . . And that he was raised on the third day according to the scriptures, and that he appeared to Cephas . . . ' John stopped again. "Who in heaven's name is Cephas?"

"I guess you're more familiar with his name in English: Peter!" smiled Sherlock. "By the way, this is one of the strongest signs that this is a very old tradition, dating back to the time when Peter was known only by his Aramaic name."

John went back to the passage again: "Let's see, where were we . . . ? 'he appeared to Cephas, then to the twelve. Then he appeared to more than five hundred of the brothers and sisters at one time, most of whom are still alive, though some of them have fallen asleep. Then he appeared to James, then to all the apostles.'"

"And then Paul wraps the whole thing up by describing that last of all, Jesus appeared also to him," interjected Sherlock.

"OK . . . " John found it difficult to make sense of the situation. "So what do you make of this?" John put away the Bible and leaned back in his armchair.

---

34. The whole passage is found in 1 Corinthians 15:3–8

"This is where material from other scholars has been of invaluable use to me," explained Sherlock. "A vast majority of scholars argue that this passage contains the oldest existing Christian creed. Our job is obviously to discern whether the information in this creed seems reliable or not—and here the time perspective is of vital importance."

Sherlock jumped up from the sofa and walked over to the window facing the street. "Allow me to illustrate: Let's say that this spot by the window is the moment when Jesus dies on the cross. Probably 30AD."[35] Sherlock then rushed through the flat and all the way out into the stairwell. John followed along, though not really with the same enthusiasm.

"Now let's assume that this is the year that Paul writes this letter to the church in Corinth—at a rough estimate in 55AD. This makes a distance of 25 years, right?"

John nodded: "Still, it's quite some time away if you are to remember all facts."

"So it may seem, replied Sherlock. "However, it's still very close to the events, if we compare to other ancient sources. For instance, we know a good deal about Alexander the Great, don't we?"

"I don't think I could recall that much about him offhand," admitted John. "But still, there are plenty of books about him, and so on. He's obviously a well-known person."

"Exactly," smiled Sherlock. "So, can you guess how long after his death we find the earliest source to his life?"

"At least as late as this, I suppose?"

Sherlock pointed out through the staircase window. "We would have to take a stroll through the next block in order to get to the correct spot in this analogy of mine. The closest source to Alexander is 300 years away!"

"Dear me . . . " John was a bit taken aback by this information. Sherlock allowed the information to sink in before he carried on: "What we need to clarify is what year this material *dates* from. This allows us to move further back. Paul writes this in 55 AD, but he claims to have given them this message when he visited the city, which was four years earlier. So we need to get back into the entrance hall again."

John followed him along through the entrance door, and closed it.

---

35. Sherlock's illustration is, to a large extent, borrowed from Gary Habermas, who has used a similar explanatory model. See http://www.veritas.org/talks/historical-evidence-jesus-resurrection-even-skeptics-believe/?view=presenters&speaker_id=1969

"Now, remember Paul explains that he gave them *what he had received*. The central question is: when did he receive this information—and from whom?"

Sherlock took some strides inside the flat, through the entrance hall and into the living-room, where he stopped beside the armchair by the coffee-table. "Scholars of all brands state that Paul got this information around 35 AD."

"That's just five years after the cross!" exclaimed John. "How do they reach that conclusion?"

"You may remember that Paul had his overwhelming experience on the road to Damascus, probably somewhere around two years after the crucifixion," answered Sherlock. "He writes in another letter that he thereafter travelled to Arabia, and then back again to Damascus.[36] Three years passed by before he went up to Jerusalem to meet the other apostles, and he writes that at this occasion he spent two weeks interviewing Peter and James. I'm sure he must have been dying to check his own experience with their testimonies of what they had seen!"

Sherlock held up his hand towards the window. "There's where it all happened. When Paul receives the creed we're just five years away from the events in question."

"Though . . . " John thought for an instant. "If Peter and James gave this creed to Paul in 35 AD, this meant that . . . they had it before him!"

"Bull's eye!" Sherlock clapped his hands together. He took some demonstratively slow steps, and with a dignified bearing took a large stride, up into the swivel chair just by the window.

"When I saw this, I almost flipped out," explained Sherlock from his elevated position. "This creed is an oral source that goes back to just one or a few years after the cross. Now, whether the information is correct, that is still a matter to be solved, but we now *know* that shortly after the death of Jesus there was a clearly formulated and established tradition about the events following Jesus' crucifixion, including a number of named people, who all claimed that they'd met Jesus alive after the resurrection."[37]

---

36. The course of events is described in Galatians 1:17–19. Galatians is, by the way, another one of those letters that the scholarly world agrees has a genuine Pauline authorship.

37. The view that this creed was established as early as within one year after the crucifixion is accepted by scholars with differing views concerning the resurrection, such as Bart Ehrman, Richard Bauckham och James Dunn.

Sherlock cautiously stepped down from the swivel chair, and they once again took their seats by the coffee-table.

"I'll willingly admit that this was news to me," admitted John. "I've read several people who, quite the reverse, argue that the resurrection is some kind of legend of a much later date."

"Pure cock-and-bull stories, with no historical support at all. All facts point towards the fact that the disciples very soon after Jesus' death—*for some reason*—began to preach that they'd met the risen Jesus," summarized Sherlock.

John reflected over the situation, read through the passage once more, and came up with yet another point: "Isn't there another important detail here? Paul mentions that most witnesses were still alive twenty-five years later, when he wrote his letter. Isn't that an indirect way of saying that it would be possible to pose critical questions to them?"

"A good observation, John. Whenever it's possible to check information, the chance that someone would dare to fabricate a story becomes radically more remote. But did you think of one other important detail? Can you see any common feature with the named witnesses in this creed?"

John scratched his head. "They're all . . . Jewish?"

"They are. And above all: they're male! You remember that when someone in this culture wished to strengthen the credibility of a statement, they always quoted male witnesses. It's evident that this creed named only those witnesses that people would find most credible."

This time it was John's turn to light up. "So your implicit point would be that . . . " He hesitated for a second, but soon carried on: " . . . as the people behind this creed decided to make it as credible as possible by only naming the male witnesse—this simultaneously underlines the strength of the information about the empty tomb, as the first reported witnesses there were women!" John felt so exhilarated that he repeatedly pushed his index finger onto the closed Bible while he spoke.

"Excellent!" cried Sherlock enthusiastically.

"Elementary," replied John with pretended relaxation and sank back in his armchair.

"Not too difficult to give the correct answer when it's placed right under your nose," mumbled Sherlock. "As always, the real trick is to ask the right questions."

Sherlock took out his mobile and quickly texted a message to Alex Barkley:

<Close to a solution. See u tomorrow>

"But . . . shouldn't you clarify that it's the ancient case you think you're on the way of solving?" objected John. "So that the man doesn't lie awake all night, hoping for a lost cross?"

Sherlock merrily smiled back and started going through the books on the coffee-table. "May I quote our acquaintance Pilate: 'What I have written, I have written!'"

With a determined expression, the detective took the book from the top of the pile, put up both his feet on the table, opened the book and put it up in front of his face.

"Now, let's see if one can get some peace and quiet to study here at home as well!"

John felt a bit offended by the taunt, gave his flatmate an irritated, though unobserved look, got up and took the stairs down to the street level. Outside the front door, he stopped in order to decide what to do next, but couldn't really figure out which way he wanted to take. It was undeniably interesting to follow Sherlock Holmes in his work. There were most certainly some areas where he'd become a bit wiser than before. In other areas, though, he still felt as if he was fumbling around in an impenetrable mist.

CHAPTER 14

SEARCHING FOR GRAVE ROBBERS

JOHN HAD BEEN OUT so late that Sherlock apparently had gone to bed when he returned home again. The following morning, John chose to leave the flat as early as he could. Right now, he just didn't feel like having any long discussions with the man who happened to be registered at the same address as he. He could take Sherlock's general bohemian traits of character, but when his harsh attitude also affected others, John felt that he'd rather vanish than begin an open argument.

Sometime after noon, John realized that he had to get back home to give some support at the scheduled meeting. The sun spread its rays over the streets of London, and spring strollers began to take off their warm outer garments and welcome a warmer season. John turned from Marylebone Road into Baker Street. With the mid-day sun shining on his back, he thought it fit to take off his coat and fold it over his arm.

He suddenly caught the eye of Alex Barkley, who was coming from the opposite direction, also in his shirtsleeves. They met just by the entrance with the number 221B.

"This is starting to become a habit, I think? Meeting right here, I mean," Alex greeted him in high spirits. "By the way, do you have an idea of what to expect during the next few hours?"

"I've learnt never to guess what to expect when Sherlock Holmes is involved," replied John dryly, and opened the door to his guest. "We'll just have to see where the journey goes. After you, Reverend!"

Up in the flat they were met by a well-dressed and quite merry detective.

"Welcome, gentlemen—allow me to invite you to a small *diné* here today!"

"Well, I took the last piece of pizza two days ago," mumbled John, but then to his surprise realized that Sherlock had laid the table nicely for three people. On the coffee-table was both china and a steaming pot with accompaniments.

"To be frank, I thought Jewish food would have fitted the situation best," explained Sherlock. "The problem is that I have a hard time with all those kosher rules, so I went with Lebanese instead. This is *Shish tawouk*—grilled chicken from the restaurant down by the corner. I hope it will suit the company."

Neither Alex nor John could come up with a good response, so they just sat down and began to help themselves to the food before them.

"So, before we move on to other matters, I'd just like to take up one issue first," began Sherlock. "I've got a tangible proposal concerning a date. How about trying to return your lost cross . . . shall we say Thursday next week? That would leave us ten more days till Easter, which hopefully ought to be enough time to solve our other case as well." Sherlock spoke without any drama at all in his voice, and heedlessly went over to showing the small bowls on the table. "Do taste these too. This walnut sauce is particularly delicious."

Alex put down his knife and fork on his plate.

"I've heard about your methods before, but it's kind of . . . different when the matter concerns you personally," he explained and looked seriously at the man, whom he still wasn't sure whether to view as a co-worker or a competitor. "I must admit that I feel rather annoyed by not having seen any signs of my case moving forward at all. How am I to be convinced that things are actually going in the direction you say?"

Sherlock finished chewing and pointed with his fork towards John. "You're welcome to ask the man over there how often I'm mistaken at this stage in an investigation."

Alex looked inquiringly over at his neighbour at the table. John replied in a calm voice: "I have never to this day experienced a situation where Sherlock has failed to present a solution to a case when he's promised to do so." John then turned to his flatmate, and said in a firm tone. "Nevertheless, there's a first time for everything, so it wouldn't hurt to show a little humility, would it?"

Sherlock continued with a moderate smile: "It seems that we're ready to proceed then? Thursday next week it is. Do have some more food, by the way, we shouldn't let it go to waste."

Sherlock filled up his plate with some more chicken. The others followed his example. It seemed apparent that the detective didn't intend to give any further information on the missing cross. The two lunch guests didn't have to wait long before Sherlock turned to a much older disappearance: "Then I have another small matter I thought we might try to solve: *What happened to the body?*"

"I understand that you've already discussed how the sources describe the linen cloth being left in the tomb, while the body itself was missing," Alex Barkley began his response. He still felt some disappointment over not having received any more information about his own missing item. However, his academic pride urged him to share his area of expertise.

"There are those who claim that the shroud of Turin, which carries a remarkable imprint of what seems to be an executed man, is the very same piece of cloth that Jesus was buried in," remarked John. "What's your opinion?

"I'd say there are a few reasons to believe that the shroud could be authentic," explained Alex calmly. "But even if this should be the case, it's still no conclusive point in the question of what actually happened to the body. What's more important are the oral testimonies that were later written down in the book of Acts, the written reports in the gospels, and above all: the early creedal tradition."

"I know the creed in 1 Corinthians 15 both forwards and backwards by now," commented Sherlock. "We know that the tomb was empty, and we have to accept as a fact that a number of people testified that they'd met the risen Jesus sometime after his death.[38] These are the facts that we'll have to explain sooner or later. We've also learnt enough about Jewish society in the days of Jesus to be able to evaluate alternative explanations."

---

38. World renowned scholar Gerd Lüdemann—a convinced atheist—admits that this is what the disciples actually experienced (even if he rejects their experiences as mere visions): "It may be taken as historically certain that Peter and the disciples had experiences after Jesus' death in which Jesus appeared to them as the risen Christ." Lüdemann, Gerd *What really happened to Jesus? A Historical Approach to the Resurrection* (Westminster John Knox Press 1995) p 80

Sherlock slowly lifted his glass, drank a sip, resolutely put the glass down on the table and said: "Therefore, let's now without mercy start dealing with what may actually have happened to the body."

"One alternative is obviously that some of Jesus's enemies got cold feet and carried away the body," began John.

"That's definitely a possibility," answered Sherlock. "However, I have one important objection: What motive could they possibly have had?"

John continued chewing while he thought. "Well, I guess you could imagine any motive whatsoever. Internal disputes among Roman or Jewish leaders, a follow-up plan that went wrong, or . . . dear me, why not a pure act of panic?"

"I've considered these possibilities—and a couple of others," replied Sherlock. "But none of them give enough of a motivation for such a drastic action. Both Roman and Jewish enemies had achieved their ultimate goal: to get rid of Jesus. In order for this alternative to hold, we need a reason for them to go one step further and steal the body."

Alex broke into the conversation: "We have to keep in mind that Jesus' enemies had prior experience of similar events in the past. They knew that earlier Messianic movements used to vanish pretty quickly, once their leader had died.[39] Politically speaking, it would have been complete madness for them to intervene in the natural process when the movement around Jesus of Nazareth soon would have disappeared just like all the others."

"I have one extra question here: Do you think that there actually was a guarding force at the tomb?" wondered John.

"Matthew writes about some kind of guard at the tomb, and I think there are good reasons to accept this information," replied Alex. "Still, Matthew is the only source to mention this, so this is not a crucial part of the train of evidence. Also: a motive to steal the body doesn't depend on whether there were any guards at the tomb or not."

"However, there's one central detail in Matthew's description of the guards' return and report of the missing body," Sherlock interjected. "And, I might add, this detail is equally important, regardless of whether there actually were any guards on duty or not."[40]

---

39. Luke mentions two such cases when retelling a speech by the famous rabbi Gamaliel. In Acts 5:36–37 he names two such leaders: Theudas and Judas the Galilean, whose movements quickly fell to pieces after their deaths.

40. The conversation depicted in Matthew 28:11–15

Sherlock pushed away his plate and wiped his mouth. The others had also finished, and cleared the table in order to focus entirely on the conversation.

"I don't get it," objected John. "If the information isn't watertight, why should we pay any attention to it here and now?"

"The main thing isn't whether the exchange of words between the high priests and the guards is correct, word for word," answered Sherlock. "The important point is that Matthew connects to the version that came to win the information war, so to speak."

Alex gave a nod of assent. "Correct indeed. Matthew states that the high priests bribed the guards to spread the rumour that the disciples had stolen the body while the guards were asleep. And then he adds: 'And this story is told among the Jews to this day.'"[41]

"Can you see the significance of this, John?" Sherlock asked enthusiastically.

John began to think intensively. He was never pleased when Sherlock made him feel foolish by asking this type of rhetorical questions.

"I guess that the reasonable answer would be . . . " John searched for the right words. ". . . that Matthew couldn't have used this phrase if another version had won what you call the 'information war.'"

"Exactly," smiled the detective. "If Matthew had referred to a completely different explanation than the one that most Jews had accepted at the time, then his gospel as a whole would have lost all credibility.[42] However, the reference to this rumour that the disciples stole the body is also an indirect confession of two other crucial points. Isn't that so, reverend?"

Alex smiled widely and gave Sherlock an appreciating nod.

"I have to admire your analytical abilities—even when they concern historical matters. It took me years to deduce as much as you've done in just a few weeks."

Sherlock Holmes just sat relaxed in his armchair and seemed to enjoy the praise.

"It's out of the question that the disciples themselves should have spread the rumour that they had abducted the body," continued Alex. "The rumour must therefore have arisen behind enemy lines. However, when Jewish leaders claim this, they also silently admit two other things."

---

41. Matthew 28:15

42. This especially as Matthew is the gospel writer who most clearly addresses Jewish readers as his primary target group.

Alex leaned forward to give some extra emphasis to his point. "Firstly: the tomb was empty. Otherwise the enemies would gladly have displayed Jesus' decaying body, thereby immediately destroying the rumour of a resurrection. And secondly: they couldn´t display the body, and had *no idea* of where it had gone, despite the fact that the message of the resurrection spread with massive speed during the years after the crucifixion."

Sherlock emphatically slammed both his fists on the table. "There are no signs, and also no alternative accounts claiming that Jesus' enemies might have stolen the body. There's no motive, and the enemies indirectly admit that they have no clue as to where the corpse is. Therefore, as long as no other information turns up, we have to consider this door closed."

He rose to his feet and stretched out his tall body. "Let's leave the dishes for now. How about taking a walk and some fresh air, while we continue to discuss further options?"

Chapter 15

WHO DEVISES PLANS?

SHERLOCK LED HIS COMPANY to the end of Baker Street and into Regent's Park. The gardeners in London had done an amazing job; tulips and forget-me-nots were blossoming in the flower beds, and made their walk a wonderful scenery of nature and beauty. The three men walked in silence, until they had passed over the small bridge over the long and narrow Boating Lake. Here, John began the conversation anew:

"I apologize for marring the atmosphere, but if we assume that the enemies of Jesus may be excluded as possible grave robbers, couldn't there be some kind of middle ground here?"

Sherlock looked amusedly at his companion.

"I mean, before we get into the alternative with the disciples themselves as possible culprits," continued John hurriedly. "Isn't it possible that some people that were *neither* downright enemies *nor* followers somehow stole away the corpse, and thereby gave rise to the rumour about the resurrection?"

"That's a serious alternative, absolutely," replied Sherlock. "But there is an important counter-question here as well: Where is the motive?"

"Well, maybe there was no particular motive at all? Maybe it was just a prank, maybe some highwaymen who thought they'd found something valuable, or whatever?"

"Excuse me for intervening," said Alex. "You know, I've studied most of the prominent scholars in this field, and I haven't seen any serious report presenting any evidence that 'somebody' stole Jesus' dead body for 'some' unknown purpose. And what is more important: nobody seems to have suggested this possibility at the time either. Instead they used the more problematic alternative that the disciples stole the corpse."

"I just have to return to the question of the motive," continued Sherlock, meanwhile a rowing boat with a young couple passed on the lake on their left, happily unaware of the rather odd conversational topic that was being discussed just nearby.

"My experience tells me that nobody takes on a criminal mission— especially not of such a bizarre nature as this—without having some kind of intent. And this almost always deals with one of two things: glory or money."

"Can you support that claim from criminal history, or are you simply guessing?" asked John sceptically.

Sherlock laughed. "Well, corpse-snatching is not the most usual trick among criminals, I'll admit that. However, there's one interesting parallel case: Are you gentlemen familiar with the attempt to steal President Lincoln's corpse from his tomb?"

Neither John nor Alex could help but smile at the example.

"You're joking, right?" replied John hesitantly.

"By no means. The event is well documented in US criminal records. A quite extraordinary story."[43]

At this moment, the three men came into a kind of glade in the park, wherein an outdoor theatre stage was erected. The company sat down on the grass in front of the stage to hear the rest of this seemingly very peculiar narrative.

"I'll try to cut a long story short," began Sherlock. "There was a criminal gang leader called Big Jim Kennally, who assembled a group to attempt to steal President Lincoln's corpse from its coffin, which in its turn was placed in a large marble sarcophagus."

"Hang on a second, was this also just a short while after his death?" asked John curiously.

"Not at all. This was eleven years after the death of the president. Now, the plan was to strike during the presidential elections in 1876 when both the public and the police were busy with other things."

"What an incredibly weird plan!" exclaimed John. Alex also took his part in the discussion: "Alright then, what motive could this Big Jim possibly have had for such a strange act?"

43. This story is described in several sources, e.g. the documentary film *Stealing Lincoln's Body*, available at http://topdocumentaryfilms.com/stealing-lincolns-body

"A very important question. Two motives," explained the detective. "If they could manage to get hold of Lincoln's remains, the plan was to use them to negotiate the release of one of Big Jim's cronies from prison, as well as exact a ransom of 200 000 dollars."

It was evident that Sherlock enjoyed retelling this kind of obscure criminal act from the past.

"Were their plans successful?" asked Alex, in amused curiosity.

"A complete disaster!" cried Sherlock triumphantly. "This was one of the worst conceived plans in criminal history. They had brought the wrong tools, and when they actually managed to crack open the sarcophagus, they could hardly move the coffin, which weighed some 250 kilos. Finally, the gang gave up and sent one of the members to cover their tracks."

"So how do we know what happened?" objected John,

"The thing was that this gang member was a double agent for the Secret Service, so instead of helping his accomplices, he summoned the police, and within twenty-four hours the whole group were behind bars!"

Alex and John laughed heartily and burst into spontaneous applause.

"Well, don't thank me," waved Sherlock deprecatingly. "Send your appreciation to the American intelligence service. It's rare that the British police perform their job as well . . . "

The little audience finished laughing, and John returned to their main subject: "So your point with this Lincoln case is that plans don't always turn out as people wish, but that someone that takes on such a peculiar task as to steal a famous person's corpse doesn't do so without a real intent?"

"Yes, I think it's an excellent illustration," explained Sherlock. "Therefore, we may for several good reasons leave the suggestion that somebody by mere mistake or just for fun would have stolen Jesus' body. Roman soldiers and Jewish leaders might not have been as cunning as Secret Service agents. But they were no fools."

"And neither were the ordinary inhabitants of Jerusalem at the time," added Alex. "The religious and political leadership obviously realized this. They would never have taken the risk of trying to give rise to a completely incredible rumour if they'd had any better at hand. We may therefore conclude that the alternative that the disciples stole the body was the strongest they had."

While they were speaking, some workers came up on the theatre stage in front of them and started cleaning the stage floor and scenery. The afternoon was getting late, and John imagined it would soon be time to leave.

"This means that we may possibly be at the heart of the matter," he said resolutely. "Could you—as a scholar—summarize how you view this alternative today?"

"It's a very important point that we now face," Alex replied in a serious tone of voice. "What we first have to understand is what frame of mind Jesus' followers must have been in after the crucifixion. They had invested their lives in a man they thought was God's chosen one, the man that the prophets had promised would come and restore Israel and also in the longer perspective: the whole world. And then . . . "

He took a deep breath, as if to give himself the chance to take in the trauma they would have experienced.

"And then came the catastrophe. The proclaimed Messiah died! And not in just any way, but through public execution in the most humiliating way known at the time. We can hardly imagine the depths of despair that his followers must have felt when they finally managed to fall asleep late that Friday night."

The two listeners remained respectfully silent for an instant, until John broke the silence: "But isn't it plausible that the disciples still nurtured a faint hope that Jesus would somehow conquer death? The gospels claim that he actually predicted this while he was alive," remarked John.

"Correct," replied Alex. "However, the gospel authors also point out that the disciples never really understood what he meant."

"A critical detail," interposed Sherlock. "Accounts that portray the narrator in an unfavourable light considerably increase the credibility of the information."[44]

"Not just for that reason," continued Alex. "A lot of research has been done on Jewish beliefs about resurrection in the days before and around Christ. Most Jews believed that God would raise everyone at the last day, but there's no text before the New Testament that speaks of a resurrection before the end of the world."[45]

"We may therefore conclude that even the disciples viewed the cross as the end of the Jesus movement?" summarized John.

---

44. For more information on the historical credibility in Jesus predicting his death and resurrection, see Licona, Michael R. *The Resurrection of Jesus: A New Historiographical Approach* (IVP Academic 2010) p 284–295

45. NT Wright gives a summary of the research on this issue. See Wright, NT "Jesus' Resurrection and Christian Origins" *Gregorianum*, 2002, 83/4. Electronic version: http://ntwrightpage.com/Wright_Jesus_Resurrection.htm

"No doubt. If anyone of them had the strength for one positive thought, it would have been the same that almost all Jews hoped for: a final resurrection of the whole creation at the last day.[46] No, the moment that Jesus died was to his followers also the death of all their hopes of him as the Messiah."

Sherlock nodded thoughtfully. It was time to get to the crucial question.

"I see. So, among your colleagues, how large is the support for the hypothesis that the disciples stole the body?

"This might come as a surprise to you—but the fact is that this hypothesis is almost completely dead in the scholarly world today."[47]

Silence once again fell on the lawn. The only thing that was heard was the scene workers, still rummaging about before the evening's performance. Sherlock decided to rephrase his question: "Just to clarify: I'm not asking what your resurrection-believing colleagues think. What do those scholars say that reject the resurrection?"

Alex continued in the same calm voice as before: "All fractions have the same opinion here, regardless of personal beliefs. The idea that the followers would have gone from complete hopelessness, then intentionally decide to steal the corpse, and thereafter travel around the Roman empire and give their lives to preach a deliberate lie that Jesus had been raised from the dead, this is so far-fetched that virtually all scholars have nowadays dismissed it."

Sherlock Holmes now buried his face in his hands, but soon jumped up in frustration and shouted out over the outdoor arena: "Come on, what is this? Somewhere there must be a solution!" His words echoed back from the amphitheatre-resembling rows of seats. He put his hands around his mouth in order to create a larger acoustic effect for his frustrated shouts. "Or is everything just a play? Only new sceneries behind the sceneries?"

The workers looked up in surprise at the loud afternoon visitors.

"Mister Detective . . . " Alex Barkley's calm voice was a clear contrast to the echoes which had just rung out. "You might perhaps be interested in the reasons why the academic world rejects this hypothesis?"

---

46. This is also how Martha understands the situation when her brother Lazarus has died, and Jesus tells her that Lazarus will be raised again: "I know that he will come back to life again in the resurrection at the last day." John 11:24

47. Craig, William Lane *Did Jesus Rise from the Dead?* (Impact 360/Kindle 2014) p 62–63

"I know precisely what the problems are," replied Sherlock with a gesture of resignation, and once more sunk to a sitting position. "I just imagined that the academic community possibly might have chosen to close their eyes to them . . . "

Alex awaited Sherlock's conclusion, without pushing him. The detective stroked his chin, sighed and continued: "This alternative suffers the same problems as your last one, John. We have absolutely no motive. You see, nobody gets the idea to steal a dead body without deriving some kind of benefit from the act. We've already mentioned the usual ones: glory or money."

John thought aloud: "And the people involved in this movement gained . . . "

" . . . not a speck of either one. Quite the contrary," Alex added. "We know that all of the apostles were willing to pay with their own life for their persistent testimony that Jesus was raised from the dead. Assuredly, some people of today may be prepared to die for strange things that they *believe* to be true. The apostles, on the other hand, died for something they *knew* was either true or false. The idea of the disciples stealing the body just doesn't fit with the facts."

The sky in the west had begun to get a tint of orange. Sherlock got to his feet. "It seems to be getting late in the afternoon. I think it's time to turn back home."

The two others followed his example, walked off and left the theatre stage to its destiny. John realized that the final act might be approaching also in their journey. He still didn't dare to predict how it was to end, though. Back on the pathway, John realized there was another detail he wished to share: "I just realized another problem with performing this kind of secret pact around a fake story—namely to keep the pact intact!"

Sherlock had by now become more relaxed, and answered with a laugh: "One almost gets the impression that you've practiced something of the kind yourself!" His smile soon vanished: "But of course, this is an almost inescapable rule in a secret plot, especially of a magnitude such as this. Sooner or later, they tend to crack!"

John could remember an episode during his first months in Afghanistan. A group of soldiers had concocted a plan to smuggle out army material with the purpose of vending to independent forces. It didn't take more than a week, though, before one of the conspirators got drunk and let his tongue run away with him. From that instant the pact was irreparably broken.

John tried to imagine how hard, not to say impossible it would have been to keep a secret such as stealing Jesus' corpse, especially when the stakes began to rise. Sherlock continued his line of reasoning: "Just think about the plot to steal Lincoln's remains. That plan cracked already before the gang could get to his coffin! How long would a collusion hold among Jesus' followers without someone leaking, consciously or by mistake? Maybe a week or two, possibly a month—if they were lucky. But a whole life, all of those involved? Unthinkable."

John thought of the doping scandals in professional cycling. The suspicions were there all the time, but the cheaters faithfully kept the net of lies intact. Well, at least for a while. It didn't take long, however, until one at a time began to reveal the truth, when they saw the rope getting tighter around their necks, until finally even the greatest star of them all found no other option but to reveal what actually happened.[48]

Sherlock went on: "So if we, despite all these problems, would propose the hypothesis that some of the disciples had entered into this kind of conspiracy, for one reason or the other, then we may be pretty certain that one of them would have betrayed his comrades in order to get something out of the affair before it all collapsed."

John shrugged his shoulders, and followed his colleague's point: "That's at least what usually happens in our time. Most probably the same behaviour would have applied also back then. I guess that's just the way humans are." This was also more or less the reaction of one of those involved, he remembered. Of course, that occasion was before the crucifixion. Thirty pieces of silver was the loot that time. Though, the gratification over that money didn't seem to have lasted for very long.

"To summarize: The hypothesis that Jesus' followers stole the corpse is thus hoist with its own petard," declared Sherlock. "It falls due to lack of motive, it falls on the practical possibility of performing such a coup, and finally it doesn't fit together with the apostle's choice to stick to their story all the way to the point of death. For these reasons, we just have to carry on searching."

Alex Barkley had remained silent during the last part of the conversation. The sun was just descending behind the trees across the narrow lake in the park. The three walkers stopped and contemplated the view. Soon, the sun had disappeared behind the tallest treetops.

---

48. The story of Lance Armstrong and the huge web of doping and lies, which unfolded step by step is told in Alex Holmes' film *Stop at nothing* (2014)

"Well, there's always a hope for a better tomorrow. Isn't that how we must think, reverend?" Sherlock said heartily and turned towards Alex. The priest hesitated with his answer. He bit his lip gently. On his cheek, a tear gleamed in the remaining daylight.

"I have to be honest with you; I don't really look forward to it that much. Sure, Easter is coming, and there's always something grand about that time of year. Still, it's no fun waking up every morning and feeling the great emptiness beside you."

He took a moment's break, and swallowed hard.

"I miss her—tremendously."

Silence fell once again. John tried to come up with something encouraging to say, but couldn't think of any suitable words.

"I fear that I've made the wrong priorities the last few years," sighed Alex. "It's not that I regret my choice of occupation. But still, trying to maintain both the calling as priest, as well as the academic career—it's taken too much time, too much energy."

"Your knowledge has been of huge assistance to us," replied John slowly.

"Still, I could have chosen not to accept every new project that turned up. Maybe that could have saved our marriage. In that case . . . it would certainly have been worthwhile."

He looked up to the sky, which was now beginning to develop a stronger tint of purple.

"Still, I guess you're correct. The sun will rise tomorrow too."

The three men resumed their walk back to the swarm and noise of the city.

CHAPTER 16

CROSS-EXAMINATION

ANOTHER COUPLE OF DAYS passed by, and Sherlock was once again as difficult to access as usual, when he was in the most decisive phase of a case. John kept himself busy networking and seeing how the land lay, as preparation before a future professional practice. One morning after breakfast he was getting ready to leave the flat, when Sherlock darted out from his bedroom.

"What means of transportation had you planned on using today?"

"I haven't really decided yet. Why, do you need a lift?"

"I received a text from Inspector Lestrade at the Yard. He wants to see me. Maybe the London police force has finally come across something more interesting than mundane assaults and petty thefts."

John looked slightly worried.

"There's an obvious risk this could mean that you won't be able to complete the two cases that you're already involved in."

Sherlock, however, seemed perfectly calm.

"I hope the solution may be quite close, for one of them. And as far as the other one is concerned, the evidence isn't likely to vanish after two thousand years. We'll solve it in time."

John realized it would be futile to carry on the discussion.

"Don't feel like driving today then, parking's too difficult. Let's take the tube over to Scotland Yard."

†

The journey from Baker Street to Westminster took no more than a few minutes. Nevertheless, John wanted to use their joint time in the underground carriage to get himself updated. He said quietly:

"As far as I can see, we seem to be somewhat stuck in explaining the empty tomb. All the same, I'm still eager to start grappling with these peculiar reports of people who claimed to have met Jesus after his burial."

Sherlock answered calmly: "What's the main problem, from your point of view?"

John looked around in the carriage. None of the morning passengers seemed to take any notice of their unusual topic of conversation. He continued: "I can accept that the creed in 1 Corinthians is very old, and shows that quite soon after the cross, people claimed that they'd met the risen Jesus. Nevertheless, I have to say that I find it difficult to accept statements like this. I mean—how do we treat a proposition as exceptional as someone claiming to have met a dead person alive and well?"

"My experience is that we initially should reject any proposition that contradicts everything we know to be true," answered Sherlock, without looking at his companion. He got up from his seat, getting ready to get off. John followed his example. In the press by the doors, the detective turned to his fellow-passenger and said in a low voice in his ear: "However, my experience also tells me that in certain occasions you may have to revise your point of view, especially when circumstances turn out to be at least equally exceptional."

"Are we really in such extreme circumstances in this case?" wondered John, looking a bit worried.

"Still too early to tell," answered Sherlock, pulled up his collar and looked straight out through the doors as the train halted at the station.

They made their way up to the street level and began the short walk to Scotland Yard. Among the people in the street, John felt compelled to take the issue one step further:

"I still can't really get over the question of how you, being the extreme sceptic you are, can even consider accepting miraculous stories in these types of faith documents?"

Sherlock sounded a bit impatient when answering: "I've tried to explain that it's not my business to scrutinize this or that miracle claim in the gospels. It's facts, pure facts, that interest me. Now, do we have reason to believe that Jesus' followers *had* an imperturbable conviction that they'd met him as risen from the dead? That's what I want to know in order to try to figure out a possible explanation for such a conviction."

John persisted: "Still, you have to agree that a critical investigation also must examine the devices which a narrator uses in order to make his audience believe his story?"

Sherlock stopped and turned to his companion. "John, do you remember The Guildford Four?"

It took John a few seconds to change mental tracks.

"Let's see . . . the gang who were convicted as IRA terrorists, but later completely acquitted after several years in jail? I think I remember having seen a film about them."

"Precisely so. A telling example of people who were convicted without enough evidence."

Sherlock resumed the promenade and carried on with the example: "Now, if you remember the film you mentioned, you might recall a striking scene. The suspected leader of the gang was cross-examined in court about the bombing that killed four British soldiers and one civilian at a pub in Guildford. He denied having performed the attack, and claimed that he had actually been elsewhere. Remember where?"

John shook his head, so the detective continued:

"He said that he couldn't possibly have committed the bombing, as he at that particular moment was in London, robbing a prostitute."[49]

John gave a laugh. "That's it! Still, I don't remember how the court valued this alibi?"

"They rejected it, and convicted the whole group, without valid evidence. One of the greatest scandals in British justice in modern time, I'd say."

"So what conclusion do you think the court should have drawn?"

"They should obviously have realized that the alibi was solid, and that therefore someone else must have conducted the terrorist attack."

"How so?" retorted John.

"For precisely the same reason that tells us why we shouldn't reject factual information in the gospels out of hand."

At these words, they reached the big sign with the inscription *New Scotland Yard*, and they came to a halt outside the entrance. Sherlock

---

49. The film, *In the name of the father* (1993), does not describe the actual course of events exactly as they were, as the suspected bomber in reality did not commit his robbery at the time that the bomb went off. The scene from the film may, however, still work as an illustration, just like Sherlock uses it here.

continued his train of thought: "Those who want to sell a false account normally try, with all their might, to appear as credible as possible. However, in cases like this, where a proponent chooses to reveal compromising details about himself, it's highly likely that he tells the truth also in other issues."

John pondered this. It did make some kind of sense. But what was the case when it came to those who testified about the resurrection? Sherlock anticipated his question: "You remember those who were counted as the chief witnesses in the early church: Peter, John, James—and the other apostles."

"Just a second," objected John. "I skimmed through the first chapters of the Acts of the Apostles the other day. There it's stated that James was executed by sword quite early on."[50]

"No, not James, John's brother. This is about James, the brother of Jesus. He is described as the leader of the church in Jerusalem, and Paul names him as a key figure, beside Peter and John."

A smile spread over Sherlock's face. "Now, if you'd want to paint a picture that would underline the exalted position of these leaders, it would be quite appropriate to portray them in rather laudatory terms, don't you think?"

"Well, that's the case with most leaders with some authority, isn't it?"

"The exciting thing is however that the gospels don't convey a particularly flattering image of these prominent figures. John, who looks so gentle and mild in the paintings, goes around asking if he may call down fire from heaven to destroy the people who don't welcome Jesus exactly the way he wishes.[51] James and his other brothers and sisters take exception to what Jesus does, and suggest that their brother ought to come home and take care of the carpentry instead.[52] And Peter—the worst of them all! What does he do? He deserts and denies Jesus on the very night when he would have needed his closest associate the most.[53] A bunch of stupid, egocentric hypocrites who chicken out when things get rough, that's the picture we get of the chief apostles before the crucifixion."

"And your point is that it's precisely these weaknesses that make the accounts worth considering?"

50. Acts 12:2
51. Luke 9:54
52. Mark 3:21
53. Matthew 26:69–75

"Exactly. It's when someone reveals their own negative sides, that you dare trust the person also in other factual information."

John looked down at the pavement, smiling: "I see. And that's the reason why you're so eager to show your own less flattering sides so often?"

Sherlock took the irony with humour: "Touché! And that's also what makes me the greatest. Especially when it comes to humility."

The detective smiled disarmingly. The sarcasm was returned, the balance restored. At the same moment, Inspector Lestrade came out through the main entrance.

"Sherlock, old chap!" Lestrade came up and greeted his old acquaintance. The consulting detective, somewhat embarrassed, shuddered.

"And John too, how nice that you could come, both of you!"

"What do you need help with today?" asked Sherlock curtly.

"Nothing at all, really, it's just been so long since we last met. I just wanted to check how things were going with you. Can I treat you to lunch? There's a really nice salad bar over there on the corner."

"Just to keep me in a good mood till the day when he really needs my assistance," hissed Sherlock between his teeth. John chuckled confirmingly.

"There are no free lunches, remember that!" he whispered back.

†

Meanwhile the company started eating their lunch, Lestrade wondered unobtrusively what the great detective might be up to at the moment.

"A missing corpse," answered Sherlock, without looking up from his salad bowl. "However, I estimate that the case is beyond your area of responsibility."

"And far beyond our own era too, I might add!" exclaimed John, without adapting himself to Sherlock's snubbing reply. He wiped his hands with the napkin. "You won't believe this, but we're deep down in the mystery of the empty tomb—belonging to Jesus of Nazareth himself!"

Lestrade responded with a loud and hearty laugh, but soon checked himself, when he realized that no other lips were forming a smile. He blushed slightly, and he had trouble finding his words: "This isn't . . . well . . . You're not serious, are you? Sherlock?"

The detective kept on chewing, and looked out into the street with a preoccupied expression. He didn't seem all that interested in dragging more people into the investigation. His zeal to proceed soon got the upper hand, though. He therefore continued where they had left off earlier.

"You know, it takes way too long to go through the whole background," he said in Lestrade's direction, and then turned his eyes towards John: "I suggest we briefly re-examine what we know about those who claimed to have met Jesus as risen. Were they male or female?"

John cleared his throat. All of a sudden, he felt like he was sitting a test, but he decided to follow along: "Those mentioned in the early creed were solely men. The gospels also name some women."

Lestrade couldn't help feeling bewildered: "Please tell me that you're just rehearsing a play or something?" Sherlock took no notice of him, and continued:

"One or several occasions?"

"If we enumerate all the reported witnesses, there would be quite a few occasions."

"Indoors or outdoors? Daytime or evening? Individually or in group?"

"All of those, as far as I can remember."

Sherlock now turned once more towards the police inspector: "Now let's say an apparently normal person comes into your office and claims to have encountered a person that you personally have seen stone dead. What would you think then?"

"I still can't believe this is happening!" cried Lestrade. "Stating the bleeding obvious, I'd first assume that the person was mentally unstable. If not so, I'd say that he had experienced some kind of illusion of aspirit or something like that."

He raised his voice: "Sherlock Holmes, what's the matter with you? Dead people don't suddenly pop round for a visit!"

"Obviously not. I'm just trying to get a grip of what's actually asserted here. However, there's one interesting detail in the context: the disciples are reported as reacting more or less the same way as you suggested now. They didn't believe it was him, but rather some kind of ghost."[54]

"A quite reasonable reaction in the circumstances, I guess," inserted John.

Sherlock nodded. "Yes. I'm actually quite surprised that the disciples are consistently described as behaving in a very rational way. But now, inspector: What would you have done if you happened to find yourself having an experience as odd as this?"

"I'd obviously step up to this vision, see and feel if it was some kind of projection or such," answered Lestrade firmly.

54. The passage from Luke 24:36–43

"A good start, that's also exactly what the texts state that Jesus asked them to do. Would that have lead you to believe your eyes?"

"I'd still assume a mix-up or something. It would have to be double- and triple-checked. At least! Dead people don't rise again, you see!" exclaimed Lestrade with vexation.

Sherlock continued in the same calm voice as before: "If we follow Luke's account, that's still the way the disciples reacted as well. They weren't fully convinced, even when they got to touch him. After all, they had seen him die! Luke then goes on to explain that they also gave him some fish, in order to further ascertain whether he could do the things a normal person can perform."

"Isn't it mentioned that Thomas does something similar?" reminded John.

"Precisely so," continued Sherlock, without taking notice of the puzzled look from the inspector who had invited them to lunch. "John writes that Thomas had been absent when the other disciples met Jesus. He didn't take their excited testimonies for granted, but said that he had to see him for himself, and touch him with his own hands if he were to believe something so exceedingly remarkable."[55]

"I still feel deeply hesitant towards throwing in any supernatural explanations," thought John aloud.

"We're not there yet," replied the detective. "Nevertheless, when I read the accounts in the gospels of how the disciples react to their rather unusual circumstances, they strike me as behaving quite cowardly when put under pressure, but at the same time quite rationally when they seem to experience something incredible. To put it short: they behave like quite normal people."

Lestrade rose to his feet so quickly that he knocked his knees into the table, which made plates and glasses rattle.

"I've followed many of your strange antics over the years, Sherlock Holmes, but this beats all I've seen so far, even from you. I truly hope that you're back to good form next time we need to solve real cases from this side of the year 2000!"

He turned round and disappeared with brusque strides. John felt slightly overwhelmed by the abrupt ending of the lunch meeting. He couldn't help but feeling a bit ashamed, even though he wasn't entirely sure

---

55. John 20:24–28

of what for. Sherlock remained just as calm as before, and cheerfully turned to his lunch partner: "So, what do you say—dessert?"

CHAPTER 17

THE CRUX OF THE MATTER

THURSDAY CAME—INEXORABLY. JOHN GAVE Sherlock a ride out to Hertford, where they had arranged a meeting with Alex at three o' clock in the afternoon. Used as he was to Sherlock's company, John was well aware of the accuracy whereby the detective used to stitch together even the most complicated cases. Still, the lump in his stomach was there all the same. He felt a deep compassion for the knowledgeable, though downhearted priest who awaited them.

Sherlock seemed to be absorbed by a volume on ancient myths about the end of the world. It was hardly time to ask any questions right now, figured John. With a bolting heart he parked the car outside the church hall and followed Sherlock the few steps up to the entrance door.

Inside, Alex Barkley awaited them as agreed. John couldn't read other people as perfectly as his companion, but the clergyman's red eyes spoke clearly to him as a doctor. The priest hadn't slept very well the last couple of nights.

"Welcome back," he greeted his visitors. His voice wasn't hard, but not as cordial as last time either. The three men sat down by the same table where they had earlier dealt with the empty tomb. Today, that felt like a long time ago, reflected John.

"So, here we are," began Sherlock resolutely. "I can see that you've been rather concerned with several things lately. I hope that today will be a day when at least some of your troubles may be resolved."

"How far afield have your inquiries led you?" wondered Alex, avoiding to pose the crucial question straight out.

"Not far. I'm pretty familiar with the fences who might be interested in an object like your lost cross, but I haven't found the need to check them out."

"How have you managed to proceed then?" replied the priest. John quietly noted that his appearance became more tensed.

"I proceeded the usual way," continued the detective calmly. "I excluded the impossible, and continued doing so until the only possible alternative remained."

"But this is still a complete mystery," exclaimed Alex. "How could a thief take out the cross without triggering the alarm, without leaving any traces, and apparently without making any efforts to sell it or hold it for ransom?"

Sherlock lowered his voice: "Simply because it never left the building."

Alex couldn't control himself, and flared up: "Are you making fun of me in my own church hall? I really don't find it appropriate to try to pull my leg in a situation like this. I think I've had my fair share of . . . "

He turned his eyes towards John, as if to seek support in a vulnerable situation. He soon realized that John looked remarkably calm, almost expectant. The priest checked his temper.

"I assume that you're playing some kind of game here. Neither we nor Scotland Yard are completely daft, you know. Obviously, we searched the surroundings high and low."

"I imagine there might be a point in searching high once more." Sherlock nodded knowingly up towards the trap-door to the attic, his voice almost exaggeratedly tranquil.

By now, both thoughts and words stuck for Alex Barkley. "But it's unthinkable that . . . " Once more he sought John's eyes for advice. This time the doctor's eyes sparkled, almost like a child waiting for Father Christmas. The priest gave up all efforts to think clearly. He rose without a word, pulled out a chair to stand on, got up to the trap-door, opened it and pulled down the stepladder from above. He looked back again at his two visitors and took a few steps up, so that his head disappeared from the guests' view. There he made a halt.

Suddenly the two men beneath could see how the priest's body gave a twitch. They could hear the man on the ladder hastily drawing his breath. Without a word he disappeared with a leap up into the attic. John looked amazed at Sherlock, who calmly remained in his chair with a moderate smile. John rushed up from his chair and up the ladder as fast as he could.

In the half-light of the attic sat Alex Barkley with a gaping mouth, staring at a large silver cross. He took it in his hands, measured its weight, turned it around, and then looked at John in a combination of surprise and shock.

"But . . . this is *impossible*! We were up here too, that day when we were searching like crazy. Then there was nothing here! Now it just lay here openly, here on the attic floor. I'm not mad, tell me I'm not mad!" He looked appealingly at John.

"May I ask for some space?" Sherlock's voice was heard from below. John quickly made room for his companion, who once again seemed to have accomplished the impossible. The ceiling in the attic was so low that they all had to keep half-bent until they could get seated more comfortably around the restored cross, which Alex still couldn't take his eyes off.

"You're completely right that it's impossible for something to just disappear, get moved or show up without a deliberate act by an active agent," began the detective. "Your conclusion is thus correct; you're not mad."

"Then tell me who in heaven's name could have put it here!"

This time Sherlock didn't reply. Instead, another, softer voice came from somewhere further into the shadows: "Perhaps someone who wished to awaken you?"

Alex reacted instantaneously. He put his hand before his mouth, and under strong emotion he whispered between his fingers: "Judith!"

From the part of the attic that was shrouded in even deeper darkness, a woman crawled out, dressed in a large shawl that covered most of her body.

Tears welled in Alex' eyes. He stretched out a trembling hand and put it gingerly on her cheek as soon as she came within his reach.

"Dearest . . . " He tried to find words. "I've missed you so terribly. But . . . "

He turned to his new acquaintances. They avoided meeting his eyes directly. He turned back to the woman opposite: "Was it *you* who . . . ?"

She nodded.

"And the cross was here in the building the whole time?"

She nodded once more.

"But . . . why?"

"Why do you think I did it?" she replied gently.

Alex, still not really able to get a hold on the situation, had trouble expressing a good answer.

"You mean to . . . in some way . . . give me a shake?"

She took his hand, looked deeply into his eyes and asked, still in a soft voice: "Have you been shaken?"

Alex nodded, and his voice broke a bit when he answered: "It took too much time and attention. All that . . . well, you know . . . Assignments, scholarly articles. All essentially good things. But I lost us along the way. I lost you."

He fell on her neck, and whispered some words into her ear. She did the same to him. They kept sitting like this for some time. Then he let go. They both wiped tears from their faces, and Alex Barkley once again turned towards the two somewhat uncomfortable onlookers.

"This was . . . without doubt the most overwhelming experience I've had in my life." He regained the strength in his voice. "Sherlock Holmes, would you care to explain how in the world this came to be?"

Sherlock adjusted himself to a more comfortable position, and began: "I realized from your initial description that this could hardly be a normal burglary. When I later received the report from your alarm system, it was evident that nobody but the ordinary staff had used their key cards the night of the crime. As no window was damaged and no secret door was to be found—oh yes, I've checked thoroughly—there were few remaining possibilities."

Mr and Mrs Barkley also took a more comfortable sitting position, a bit closer together.

"You've had enough foresight to attach an alarm chip here under the cross." Sherlock grabbed the article of value, which for a moment had almost been forgotten, and showed the little mark under the foot of the cross. "This gives the alarm if taken out through doors or windows, or if someone tries to remove the chip by force. This left few other alternatives than the fact that the cross was actually still here in the building."

"But how could you figure out the identity of the . . . culprit?" Slightly embarrassed, Alex met his wife's eyes.

"I questioned those that were on some kind of duty the night in question. I also took the chance of letting them share information about the others, rather than just posing questions about that particular night." Sherlock leaned forward and whispered, even if it wasn't really needed. "You have a rather gossipy staff, I can tell you . . . "

"Doesn't surprise me a bit!" Alex replied with a short laugh.

"Oh yes, they had plenty to reveal about each other. However, nothing they told me pointed towards any of them having any particular intent to steal or possibly hide away a treasure like this."

"But what led you to this . . . Judith here?" wondered John curiously.

"Well," replied Sherlock circumspectly. "There was something uncertain in the tone of voice of the deacon who turned on the alarm that night. Not enough to give any hard facts, but enough to raise a suspicion. As you may know, most crimes in this world are committed by close relatives, and when this happened two days after your separation, there was a clearly troubling situation connected to your marriage." The Barkleys couldn't help nodding recognizingly.

"Therefore, I went on that instinct, and quickly got hold of and memorized Mrs Barkley's phone number. It was quite nice of you to lend me your mobile last time we were here, reverend."

The priest turned down his eyes, realized that he'd been hoodwinked, albeit with a good motive: "There's me, having a pious hope that you were looking up Bible quotes from my sermon . . . "

Sherlock just smiled contentedly.

"Well then, there's a time for everything, right? So, I called and asked politely—I hope?" Sherlock looked over at Judith, whose smile gave the answer without words.

"I simply asked whether we could meet and talk. When we met, I immediately presented my suspicions, and I have to praise you for giving a more straight-forward confession than any thief I've met so far!"

Judith Barkley laughed heartily: "I just got the impression that you realized where the shoe pinched. I therefore shared my very personal frustration that we— yes, the blame is also mine—had drifted so far apart from each other that we no longer found the strength to carry on our relationship. So when I, a few days after our separation, decided to pop in after the sewing circle meeting to get things off my chest with one of the ladies from the congregation, the door was to my surprise unlocked and everyone apparently already gone home."

"And that was when you suddenly took it into your head," added Sherlock.

"Yes. Or, to be correct . . . it sort of just happened. When I realized I was alone in the building, I directed my steps up to the cross, and in frustration I grabbed hold of it. Maybe it was my husband, maybe it was God I was upset with. And then it happened."

"The cross came loose from its base, right?" thought John aloud.

"I almost fell backwards with the cross over me," confirmed Judith. "At first, I panicked for a second, but then I suddenly saw the chance of . . . well, creating a dramatic situation. Almost instinctively, I took the cross and pulled it up here to the attic. I can tell you it was heavier than I thought!" she laughed.

"This was also evident to a trained eye. If you look here, you knocked the cross right here." Sherlock pointed to a small dent on the top step of the stepladder. "There's a faint, faint trace of silver here in the dent, and it hadn't yet become discoloured when I searched the building the other week. This meant that the silver mark was fresh. The case was more or less solved."

"Then why on earth didn't we find the cross up here?" asked Alex in astonishment.

"Come over here and feel carefully with your fingers on the floor," showed Sherlock.

The priest followed the suggestion. With a concentrated look, he moved his hand back and forth over the attic floor.

"Isn't there something like a joint here?"

"Most definitely so!" Sherlock lit up. "I felt it when I made a quick investigation the other Sunday."

"I discovered this hole under the floor last year by sheer coincidence, when I was looking through old magazines that had been lying about for ages," revealed Judith. "Almost without thinking, I managed to push the cross inside it and then climb back down again. But just as I was on the way out, I met the deacon. She had just remembered that she'd left the alarm off, and was about to turn it on when I exited the hall. I couldn't think of how to act in my hurry, so I just said a short 'Good night' and vanished. I suppose she realized the connection the morning after, when the cross was found missing."

"But why, dear?" exclaimed Alex.

Judith Barkley hesitated a bit with her reply. She turned to her husband and said:

"I think that I somehow, maybe subconsciously, wanted to jolt you. Make you rethink what you value in life. Finally, when I received a last update from your new friend the detective yesterday, he could confirm that you'd really begun to revalue things."

"Absolutely. I've definitely done that."

The priest's gaze once more became slightly shiny with tears. Sherlock got up into a crouching position, getting ready to close the gathering.

"Well then, reverend—you were right. It is a beautiful cross. Hopefully, it will continue to grace your parish for years to come. I think we may hereby consider this case closed."

The pro tempore marriage therapist nodded towards John as a signal to follow him. They both climbed down and walked away towards the door, leaving the couple up in the attic and the other effects in the building to their fate.

Still in something of a daze, John looked at his companion with admiration. He was well aware of his flatmate's ability to function as a coldly calculating computer. Though these not too frequent instances where he also expressed some human empathy meant far more to raise the esteem in which he held Sherlock Holmes.

"There are times when the presence of a consulting detective is quite superfluous," said Sherlock and went out on the steps. "Let's return to Baker Street."

CHAPTER 18

TURNING POINT

ON LIGHT FEET, JOHN Watson jogged up the stairs at Baker Street. If yesterday had been a successful end to the case of the lost cross, this Friday had been a particularly good day for John. The new car went like clockwork, and really facilitated travelling to places where the underground didn't reach. During the day he'd had a good conversation with a colleague, who in times ahead might be a potential partner in a joint surgery in the northern part of the city. Maybe a more settled future was waiting around the next corner. John felt both stimulated and hopeful.

He was about to open the door, when he checked himself. Wasn't that music that he heard from inside the flat? Yes, most definitely so. He could well recognize the sound of the bowing of his violin-playing friend. It had been quite some time since he last heard Sherlock lose himself in a languorous violin composition.

He opened the door quietly and carefully peeked inside. Sherlock Holmes was in his emotional glory. Seemingly shut out from the outer world, he looked completely absorbed by the musical piece. Perhaps this is how he channels the aesthetic energy that otherwise appeared to be absent, or maybe just thoroughly concealed behind the analytical mask, thought John to himself.

With great frenzy, Sherlock completed the finale of the piece. Applause from the armchair made John jump slightly.

"Marvellous, Mr Holmes, just marvellous!" exclaimed Mrs Hudson from her seat. "The experience of listening to you is infinitely improved by actually seeing you play, not just hearing you through the ceiling."

"It's good to hear you play your instrument again, I think it's been a while," said John.

In surprise, Sherlock turned to his second listener. "Oh, John. I didn't hear you. Have you been here long?"

"Came just now—but I think I recognize the music. Still, I can't figure out what it was."

"Bach, if I'm not mistaken, right?" filled Mrs Hudson in, before Sherlock found the time to reply.

"Entirely correct. Bach remains unrivalled among composers," replied Sherlock and put his violin and bow down. "It was a part from his St Matthew Passion. I thought he might inspire us before our final round."

"You haven't started with Handel's Hallelujah Chorus then?" smiled John.

"By no means. For one thing, the violin doesn't have the melody in that piece. And secondly, I think we've got quite a bit left to go before we would dare a hallelujah."

"Well, I'm just happy that you seem to be in full vigour," explained Mrs Hudson and got up from her armchair. "I think I'll go down to my own flat and make myself some supper. But do let me know when you give your next violin concert!"

The old landlady calmly pattered out from the rooms. John took a seat in the sofa and tried to find something easy to read on the table, something not directly connected to the case of the empty tomb. He soon gave up his efforts, though, and decided that they were most probably facing another week or so of focusing on this ancient theme.

"I've been thinking about these witnesses that we discussed the other day," called John out towards the kitchen, where Sherlock seemed to be busy with something. "Certainly, they were committed to their testimony, but they're still insiders—people from Jesus' own fan club. Isn't there a possibility that someone in that position could be at risk of self-delusion?"

Sherlock came out in the living-room and sat down on the armrest, and returned the question:

"You mean that it would have been a cleverer strategy for Jesus to push off and appear to Pilate or somebody of that kind instead?"

"Why not? Well, if that option was open to him, I mean . . . "

Sherlock slid down into the armchair, indicating that he could well imagine a longer discussion on this topic. He leaned forward and lowered his voice: "John . . . What would convince you that I spoke the truth if I were to tell you that . . . I'm God?"

John couldn't hide his sudden uncertainty as to how he should deal with the question he'd just heard. Had Sherlock finally gone completely haywire and now wished to state that . . . ? Sherlock saw his companion's doubtful face, and burst into laughter:

"No, no . . . I'm not God. Not at all, actually. Rather quick-minded: absolutely. All-knowing and all-powerful: not really." Sherlock leaned back again and returned to his example. "But let's imagine that I—purely hypothetically—were to announce such a thing. Is there anything at all that would convince you?"

John smiled faintly, looked out through the window and thought for an instant before he replied: "I really don't have any idea what would, Sherlock." He looked back again at his colleague. "You see . . . I know you. Pardon me for being so straight-forward, but apart from your extreme intelligence, you don't possess that many of the qualities that are usually ascribed to God—or any earthly saint, for that matter."

"Alright, let's change the example then," replied Sherlock in amusement. Despite the straight answer, he had remarkable problems hiding his pride over the recognition of his intellectual capacity. "We'll use a slightly more saintly example than me. Let's take Mother Teresa; could she have been God?"

"She was truly a good person, Nobel laureate and so on, who did everything in her power to help the poor in India," answered John thoughtfully. "Still, this obviously doesn't mean that she's God."

Sherlock persisted with his example: "Nevertheless, there were many who really looked up to her. Couldn't we suppose that someone would claim that she was divine, for example by stating that she had risen again after her death?"

John firmly shook his head.

"It doesn't actually matter how good a person is, we're still just human. When you're dead, you're dead."

"Very true, John. Very true. But let's say that mother Teresa's tomb was empty?"

"I'd obviously assume that someone had moved her body someplace else!"

"Excellent, I agree completely. By the way, that was also the conclusion that the first discoverers of the empty tomb are stated as having drawn."

Sherlock leaned forward and picked up his old confirmation Bible from the table. "The apostle John states that when Mary Magdalene stood crying outside the empty tomb, Jesus suddenly stood there, though she didn't understand that it was him. Instead, she got the unreligious but very rational idea that it might have been the gardener who had turned up.[56] Can you recall what she said to him?"

"You tell me, you have the text there," said John.

"Well, she didn't start singing the Hallelujah Chorus either, that's for sure . . . On the contrary she seems to have acted like any other sane person would in her situation. She simply asked the man she thought was the gardener if he'd moved the body, and in that case if he could tell her where he'd laid it, so that she could fetch it back again."

"Sounds more or less like I would have reacted myself," commented John.

"I'd think so," agreed Sherlock. "Now, as we've said before, the gospels are filled with this kind of calm and reasoning response. Not even Jesus' followers went for any supernatural explanation just like that. They wanted hard evidence—just like you would have done if someone proposed that Mother Teresa was alive again after her death."

"This is actually quite soothing news," figured John. "Otherwise, you might suppose that the disciples were quite . . . er . . . simple people."

"You mean: easy to fool?"

John blushed a little bit: "Well, not exactly . . . "

"No, we humans seem to be pretty alike, regardless of time and culture." Sherlock stretched out in the armchair and comfortably put his feet up on the table. "Let's now return to my previous question how you would react if I'd claimed to be God. Here is an important example that might say more than the disciples' testimonies about the risen Jesus. You remember James, the brother of Jesus?"

"He who first didn't believe that Jesus was the Messiah?"

"Exactly, my dear fellow. There are at least two independent accounts of how he and his siblings did not support their brother's claim to divinity. Mark, whose gospel is the oldest, describes that they quite early on thought that Jesus had lost his mind, and planned to bring him back home.[57] Now,

56. John 20:11–18

57. Mark 3:21. The other example is from John 7:5, which states that "not even his own brothers believed in him."

imagine James having this brother who he thinks he's God, and James thinks that there might be something seriously wrong with him."

"I'll admit that for a brief moment I thought the same about you just a minute ago . . . " admitted John.

Sherlock smiled back with content. "So, what would make a man like James change his mind, and do it so completely that he, after his brother's death, suddenly starts preaching boldly that his brother was risen, and was in fact God himself?"

"I guess that would take a small miracle," chuckled John.

"Would a small one really do?" snapped Sherlock.

John put one leg over the other and took some moments to think before he answered. "On second thought, it would probably take a quite exceptional occurrence for someone like James to accept such a proposal. Firstly, he would have had to be sure that the deceased was actually dead, that the body was really gone and that it hadn't been moved."

"Check!" replied Sherlock. He lowered his voice: "But would it take anything more than that?"

"Dear me, what should I say!" cried John. "I guess he would have had to see his brother with his own eyes, touch him, talk to him. Basically: do everything he could to check that he was definitely, without any doubt, back from the dead."

The room became silent, until John went on: "Which means . . . pretty much like the examination we were talking about when our friend Lestrade got upset and left the other day," summarized John.

"Mmmm . . . " thought Sherlock aloud. "The problem is that we have no information at all about what a possible encounter between James and his risen brother would have been like. What we do have is the early creed in 1 Corinthians. But we still have to consider this drastic revaluation from a sceptic like James. Something really extraordinary must have caused it."

A small wrinkle of concern appeared between Sherlock's eyes: "I begin to feel that the number of possible alternatives is shrinking considerably."[58]

John's thoughts continued to spin around in his head. A sceptic as witness is obviously more valuable than a devoted follower, he thought. The ultimate source would of course be if a downright enemy had claimed to have had the same experience. Sherlock seemed to have read his thoughts:

58. Sceptical New Testament critic Hans Grass admits that the conversion of James is one of the surest proofs of the resurrection of Jesus. See Grass, Hans *Ostergeschehen und Osterberichte*, referred to in Craig, William Lane *Reasonable Faith* (Crossway Books 2008) p 380

"Now, if this applies to the sceptic James, the same thing is even more pertinent for an enemy such as Paul."

"You know, I've read the story," responded John sceptically. "I guess we'll just have to admit that we don't know exactly what happened to him there on the road to Damascus."

"You mean: apart from the fact that we normally treat people's personal accounts seriously, as long as we don't have good reasons to reject them," replied Sherlock. "Most important to our investigation, though, is the fact that Paul was transformed from an enemy who worked assiduously to stop what he considered to be a dangerous delusion, into a devoted champion of the message of the resurrection."

"And you think this requires an explanation as well?" wondered John.

"Don't you?" replied Sherlock amusedly.

John nodded reluctantly. Sherlock stood up from his armchair and walked up to the window.

"You see, this case increasingly resembles a jigsaw puzzle. We've begun to get an overview of what pieces we have, as far as pure facts are concerned. The crucial question now is what the complete picture looks like, in which all these pieces can fit together. A final picture where one or two pieces have to be put aside or trimmed to fit in, simply won't do."

"And you're not there yet?" asked John cautiously.

"Not yet." Sherlock turned around to look at his companion with a grave face. "We have one more week to work at it. I hope that'll be enough."

CHAPTER 19

A NEW DOOR OPENS

THE SILENCE IN THE flat was suddenly broken by an eager knock on the door. John felt the timing was well suited for a break in the conversation, and got up to open. Outside was a radiant Alex Barkley with an armful of roses. He fell on John's neck with one arm, and thereafter rushed straight inside, where Sherlock once again had seated himself in the armchair.

"I cannot thank you enough for your effort, Sherlock! You've rescued our cross. And more than that: you've rescued our marriage! My gratitude to you is greater than words can express."

Sherlock remained seated without looking up. He didn't look particularly annoyed or particularly glad. John watched the scene from a distance, and blushed a bit at his friend's lack of social competence. Alex seemed hesitant over Sherlock's lack of response. He stretched the bunch of flowers towards the sitting detective.

"I brought a simple gift—I hope you'll accept this as a token of our appreciation."

Sherlock still didn't look up, but at least began to speak: "John, could you check for something to use as a vase? Look among the test tubes and flasks over there in the corner."

John carefully took over the rose bouquet and bustled over to the chemistry equipment which Sherlock had stored away. He returned with a glass reservoir, which with some imagination could pass for a flower vase.

"That'll do," said Sherlock absently, then roused himself to add: "Oh, and give it a good rinse first, I used nitric acid in it last time."

John shook his head and took flowers and glass reservoir with him into the kitchen, while Alex sat down in the sofa. He still looked over-whelmingly happy. Sherlock gave him a quick glance.

"You'd saved the ring, I see."

"Well, I guess hope springs eternal," smiled the priest and looked down at his hand, where the wedding ring was back in its usual place. "Sherlock, everything is back to normal again." Alex checked himself: "No, actually: better than normal. You know, it's strange . . . I've often preached about how people grow during times of crisis. But nevertheless, it's a truth that's difficult to grasp until you're personally affected."

Sherlock still seemed to be absorbed in his own thoughts. The priest carried on his account: "I was so inspired by the recovered cross that I asked the church council if we could, as the early church used to, perform the Easter Sunday mass at the first light of dawn under the open sky, in a glade in the forest west of town. And can you imagine, they bought the suggestion!"

There was still no reaction from the man opposite. Alex tried another way to break the ice.

"So, what about your own problem? Might it be as easy to solve?"

John returned with the large rose arrangement, which he placed on the coffee-table. Sherlock's silence made him fill in the void: "As far as I see it, the pieces in the jigsaw seem more or less laid out, but the picture itself still seems unclear."

"Then I guess the next step is to walk out on the tightrope and see where it ends?" said Alex in a challenging tone.

"The doors close," mumbled Sherlock, seemingly annoyed. "They just close before me."

Alex decided to bring matters to a head: "So, how deeply have you considered the hypothesis of a supernatural intervention?"

Sherlock leaned his head backwards and gave a frustrated sigh. "I don't have a key to such a door. Sorry."

John shook his head: "And to think that a dead man just stands up and walks out . . . Too bad. That's impossible. Impossible!" he exclaimed passionately.

"Absolutely," replied Alex without an instant of hesitation. "If the universe is a closed system, where everything is controlled by the law of cause and effect, then *every* possible theory would be more plausible than the hypothesis that Jesus just got up and left." Alex took one more breath before he went on: "However, that's not what the first witnesses claimed."

"They didn't?" said both John and Sherlock with one voice.

"Let's look at the first few instances where the resurrection was preached publicly. We have four very early speeches, which were summarized, memorized and then written down by Luke."[59]

Alex could see in the corner of his eye how John drew his breath to give voice to a hesitation, and hurried to continue: "Now, you have to remember that this was an oral culture, where people were very used to memorizing and repeating messages verbatim."

The priest took up the Bible from the table. "These speeches are reproduced in the beginning of the book of Acts. Look here!" With experienced fingers, he turned to the right place."

"Here you can see that all four speeches convey more or less the same message. First, it's Peter who on the day of Pentecost speaks to the people in the street: 'You and the Romans nailed Jesus to a cross and executed him. But God raised him from the pains of death, and we are all witnesses of it.' Next time, it's Peter and John before the visitors in the temple: 'You killed the Originator of life, whom God raised from the dead. To this fact we are witnesses!' After that, Peter and John stand before the High court: 'You crucified Jesus of Nazareth, whom God raised from the dead. And it is impossible for us not to speak about what we have seen and heard.' And finally, we have the whole group of apostles questioned by the High court: 'The God of our forefathers raised up Jesus, whom you seized and killed by hanging him on a tree. And we are witnesses of these events.'"[60]

"Peter's accusations are very sharp throughout," noted John.

"You can well imagine why," replied Alex. "I think Peter dares to be this bold simply because he had himself fallen completely during the night before Jesus' death. First, he proudly declared that he would give his life for Jesus, and a few hours later he'd three times denied even knowing him."

"Still, none of these speeches state that Jesus himself suddenly got the idea to wake up and step out?" interjected Sherlock.

"Precisely my point!" responded Alex. "None of these sermons indicate that the man Jesus of Nazareth was powerful enough to rise up after death—basically because this is impossible. What Peter does state, however,

59. The fact that these sermon summaries come from a very early oral tradition, dating from the first decennium after the cross, is acknowledged also by Bart Ehrman, who rejects the resurrection. See Ehrman, Bart *Did Jesus exist?* (Harper Collins 2012) p 109–113, 140–141, 172, 232, 261–262

60. The quotations are slightly shortened and paraphrased. In their complete form they are found in Acts, chapters 2–5.

is that the eternal God shone into our world and gave new life to Jesus' dead body. One more thing, while we're at it: Peter repeats each time that he and the others were witnesses who could give first-hand accounts of their encounters with the risen Jesus."

Alex Barkley took an extra breath, and went on: "Therefore, the question isn't: Can a dead person come back to life again purely by himself? Here the answer is evidently 'no'. This leaves us with the question whether there is a theoretical and practical possibility that God exists and actively intervened to raise Jesus. As long as this possibility isn't completely closed, it must be one of the possible explanations to the events we've been discussing over the last few weeks."

This did turn the issue around, at least a little, figured John. He looked at Sherlock for a clue how they ought to proceed. The latter had pushed his hands deep into his pockets and now looked deeply worried.

"I've been trying to push this explanation aside for weeks. But now I feel I'm at the end of the alley," he said without any emotional expressions. "We can't reach any further. We don't *know* whether there is a God. Neither do we have any methods to reach a sustainable answer." Sherlock leaned his head backwards and closed his eyes. "That's it. The end—sorry."

The visiting priest chose not to rush the conversation, but let the others deliberate together.

"All the same . . . wouldn't it be a shame to drop this conundrum, now when we've actually reached this far?" objected John, apparently quite disappointed.

"Listen . . . " Sherlock looked back at his flatmate. "I entered this case deciding to perform a ruthless search for facts, plus some logical reasoning, thereby reaching a solution to the empty tomb. However, now we stand at a door that reason cannot pass. Damn it!" Sherlock beat his fist on the armrest, and dust spread around him.

John continued: "On the other hand: you knew perfectly well when you took this 'case' that it would touch upon areas where normal detective work can't reach."

Sherlock rose, and started to walk around in the room. He clenched his fists and seemed to descend into an agony of decision. Then he stopped, seemingly at some kind of turning point.

"No! I refuse to put an end to this investigation just like that! This case is far too peculiar to just leave it here." He turned to his visitor: "Now it's up to you, my dear priest! Please give your rational explanation to why you believe that God exists." He caught his breath: "I assume that a scientifically engaged man like you has such an explanation?"

Alex Barkley composedly put the Bible back on the table, laid his hands in his lap, and smiled: "It's not every day you get this kind of interesting questions, I can tell you. Not even as a priest! Do take a seat, by all means." He smiled and held out his hand in the direction of the sofa, as if to ease the heightened emotion in the room. Sherlock resigned back to his seat.

"There we are. Well, I guess you could say that my faith began to take real shape during my late teens," began Alex. "During those years I started to shake and rattle all world views and ideologies as hard as I could, to see which of them could stand the test."

"Quite the same thing that we're doing right now, concerning the empty tomb," inserted Sherlock.

"Not a bad comparison at all," commented the priest. "When I was a young man, looking for truth, I took the materialistic world view that has been so influential in our present British culture and turned it inside out. I also decided to study the philosophies of the East seriously. But in none of these world views did I find any tenable grounds. Neither could I find any reasonable answers to the great questions I had about life."

The two men listened politely, and avoided asking counter-questions.

"Still, however much I tried to tear down the Christian faith, it stood firm. It passed the test scientifically, when it came to the beginning and reason for the universe, as well as when it came to the perfectly ordered balance—all the way from the entire universe, down to the smallest building blocks of life itself. I also found that Christianity was able to stand the test when I weighed it against my intuitive sense of right and wrong, and also against the spiritual longing that has been present in all human cultures. None of these made any sense without God."

Alex didn't wish to push things, and so wrapped up his personal testimony: "These more scientific and intellectual reasons aside, I can also agree with Pascal: 'The heart has its reasons which reason knows nothing of'," he smiled and patted himself on his chest, where today a cross hung.

John kept silent, and found it more suitable for Sherlock to take the lead. The detective once again stood up, went over to the window, looked outside with a thoughtful expression, and slowly gave his response: "I can't have an opinion on that whole package. But let's for the sake of simplicity conclude at least one thing:" He turned towards his visitor: "You, an intellectual man in your prime, are earnestly convinced that there is an almighty God who has created the world. To be sure, there are rational people who hold the opposing view too. But it's also evident that a large number of other intelligent men and women share your belief."

With slow paces, Sherlock came back to the two others. "In the case before us, we therefore have to leave open the possibility—whether large or small isn't the crucial point—that God does exist. It then follows logically, that the resurrection is an alternative which still remains on the table, at least theoretically. If that's the case, it may also be weighed against the other explanatory models." Sherlock clenched his teeth: "The case of the empty tomb *must* find its solution!"

He made a rhetorical pause. "Gentlemen—the game is on, once again. What remains is: the final act."

CHAPTER 20

THROUGH THE HAZE

IT WAS MONDAY. Holy Week had begun, and the pace at the church in Hertford had calmed down after Palm Sunday's service. The spring haze that lay over the neighbourhood contributed to the muted atmosphere in the late afternoon. Outside the church hall stood the two companions from Baker Street, waiting for their host, who had promised to come and let them in. Sherlock looked at his watch and grumbled with some irritation:

"Five past five. Can you imagine that people can't learn to keep an appointment!"

Soon thereafter, a car turned into the parking lot with some speed, and parked on its spot. Out of the driver's seat jumped Alex Barkley. From the passenger side his wife simultaneously stepped out.

"I do apologize, I hope you haven't had to wait too long," Alex excused himself, while trying to find his key card from the inside pocket of his coat, which swung gently around him in the light breeze.

John felt joy springing up within him, when he saw the Barkleys together.

"I thought it might be a good idea for all involved to have another person join in our current project," smiled Alex, while unlocking the door to let his guests inside.

Sherlock's face revealed a mix of pride and uncertainty before the new acquisition to their temporary working team. Still, he didn't give voice to his opinions.

The company entered a side room in the church hall, where the candidates for confirmation used to gather. The tables and chairs were quite shabby. In the front was a traditional teacher's desk and a big blackboard.

"I have to apologize once more, for the ageing furniture," said Alex, slightly embarrassed. "The church council have just made a decision to . . . "

"Nothing to apologize for," interrupted Sherlock firmly. "You know, this is an ancient problem we're dealing with. It would have been strange to try to sum up this case in a high-tech environment."

The detective took the role of seminary leader and stationed himself behind the teacher's desk. The others sat down as listening participants.

"Now then, it feels good to be able to gather all of us here today, newcomers as well!" Sherlock nodded towards Judith. "Today I'd like us to do our best to produce a final compilation of what we actually *know* about the events that Passover some two millennia ago."

Sherlock took up a piece of chalk, and began to write. On top of the left side of the blackboard he wrote the headline *Facts* and on the corresponding place on the right side, he wrote *Possible explanations*. Thereafter he turned round to his small audience and began in a solemn voice:

"We have less than a week till Easter. The case is approaching its final phase. Let's therefore analyse which pure facts we have to start out from. No free speculations—we'll start with what we actually know. Thereafter, we may search for solutions. Is that OK with you?"

His listeners nodded eagerly. Sherlock raised the chalk and got going:

"Number one: Jesus died on a cross." Sherlock wrote rapidly with a rather sprawling hand. He turned to the others: "Anyone against"

"Well, there were several people against it back then, but they still couldn't stop the Romans from executing him," smiled John.

"Alright then, we may consider this proven beyond all doubt," continued Sherlock and started to write again. "Point number two: Jesus was laid in a known grave. Everyone still with me?"

They all nodded.

"All sources agree, and there are no opposing accounts. We're on very safe ground here," commented Alex. "We might also add that several of the gospels underline, in slightly different words, that Jesus' women followers were watching while Joseph of Arimathea buried Jesus in the rock tomb."

"You mean that this would render it unthinkable that they had mistakenly just gone to the wrong tomb on Sunday morning?" wondered Judith. Her husband nodded contentedly.

Sherlock went on with his lecture.

"Thirdly: After the death of Jesus, his followers had lost all hope."

"Now, this is incredibly important background information, in order to understand the situation," mentioned Alex. "The despair of the disciples is mentioned in the gospels, although somewhat indirectly.[61] Jewish sources from the time are on the other hand very clear: the Messiah that people expected would be a strong king who was supposed to free the Jewish people from external oppression. Nobody expected a Messiah who died. And nobody expected a resurrection from the dead before the last day. They all realized that the death of Jesus was the end of all they had hoped for."

"This now leads us to the very heart of the enigma," continued Sherlock. "Some days after the crucifixion, Jesus' tomb was found empty!" The detective smacked the dot in the exclamation point so hard that a cloud of dust came from the chalk.

"Could we repeat how we know that the tomb was actually empty?" asked John.

"Of course." The priest cleared his throat: "One: we have four distinctly independent sources in the gospels, we have the oral sources in the form of Peter's sermons from the time after the cross, and we have the early creed that Paul quotes in 1 Corinthians."

"Just a second," objected John. "That passage doesn't explicitly mention the empty tomb, does it?"

"Correct," continued Alex. "Indirectly, though. The creed states that Jesus was buried, and thereafter appeared before a number of named people. We must also keep in mind that this modern idea of some kind of 'spiritual resurrection' didn't exist at all in Jewish thinking. If someone was buried, and then was claimed to have been resurrected, it explicitly meant that the body no longer remained in the tomb."

"It brings to mind a case we had," thought John aloud. "Do you remember the man with the twisted appendix, Sherlock?"

A smile spread across the detective's lips. John turned to the others. "To make a long story short, Scotland Yard had arrested a man after a big drug deal. However, he seemed to have a watertight alibi, because medical journals showed that he at the time in question was under anaesthetic, having his appendix removed."

---

61. John 20:20 mentions that the disciples hid for fear of the Jews, Luke 24:21 describes the forlornness of the two disciples on their way to Emmaus.

"It's quite easy for an experienced forger to borrow the identity from an unsuspecting hospital patient!" remembered Sherlock in a merry voice. "The whole thing was obviously quite simple to solve. Still, it would have been quite hilarious if a prosecutor had carried the case further, arguing that the man's body could have been asleep in hospital, but that his spirit at the same time could have been at a parking lot, conducting dirty business," chuckled the detective.

"A striking parallel," continued Alex. "We must also keep in mind that body and soul were even more closely coupled together in Jewish thought. Nobody would have come up with the weird idea that Jesus was risen, if his body still remained in the tomb. Another important support for the empty tomb is of course that the first reported witnesses were women. Because of the low status of female witnesses, nobody would have been so stupid as to state such a thing, if it hadn't been true."

John was uncertain if the expression with which Judith looked at her husband reflected dismay or appreciation. Alex went on: "Also, we have no competing accounts contradicting the empty tomb. The only thing we have from the years thereafter is the much weaker suggestion that the disciples stole the body. The fact that this story came not from the followers of Jesus, but from the enemy camp, gives an even stronger support for the reliability of the matter. If the tomb hadn't been empty, this rumour would obviously have been pointless. And finally: the resurrection was preached publicly less than two months after the crucifixion in the very city where Jesus had been executed. If there had been even a remote possibility that Jesus' remains were still in the tomb, this movement would have burst like a balloon immediately."[62]

"We can firmly establish that the tomb was empty," summarized Sherlock. "Now, point five: Shortly thereafter, Jesus' followers began to preach that they had met him as risen. Dr Barkley, please fill in."

Alex sat comfortably leaned against the backrest with his arms crossed.

"Scholars are united on this issue, regardless of whether they believe in the resurrection or not. The disciples were preaching that Jesus was alive, and they personally testified that he'd appeared to them as risen from the

---

62. Church historian William Wand puts it like this: "All the strictly historical evidence we have is in favour of [the empty tomb], and those scholars who reject it ought to recognize that they do so on some other ground than that of scientific history." Wand, William *Christianity: A Historical Religion?* Quoted in Habermas/Licona *The case for the Resurrection of Jesus* p 73

dead. How they actually got this impression, that's the next step. But there is no doubt: this is what they experienced, and this is what they preached."[63]

"Which takes us directly to our next point," said Sherlock and went on writing: "The disciples were fully convinced that their message of the resurrection was true."

"One might think that this is a superfluous point about people reporting something they've experienced," Alex added. "Still, experience shows that people sometimes spin the truth. Nevertheless, keeping to a false story can be very trying. When put under pressure, people usually retreat if they've lied deliberately, and also if they just feel some slight uncertainty. The thing here was that all of the disciples held on to their testimony of having met the risen Jesus, and they continued to do so through persecution, through torture and to the point of death."[64]

By now, there was just a small space left on the bottom left side of the blackboard. There Sherlock added the last point. "Finally then, point seven: Sceptics like James, and enemies like Paul also testified to having met the risen Jesus."

"And this is an important point because . . . ?" asked Judith.

"Simply because proponents of a cause—at least in theory—could be suspected of deluding themselves in order to defend the message they preach," clarified Alex. "However, it would take something very special for a brother who'd earlier rejected Jesus, and an enemy like Paul to suddenly—with their lives at stake—start preaching that they'd met the risen Jesus. It would take a quite extraordinary event."

"There, my friends, we have the facts written down before us!" concluded Sherlock. "Shall we have a tea break before we get into the really tough part—trying to reach a valid explanation?"

"We can manage," exclaimed Judith Barkley excitedly. She smiled: "I speak for my husband too!"

63. In a survey of all scholarly articles in this subject since 1975, Gary Habermas explains that hardly any fact in this matter is more widely recognized today than that the early Christians had real experiences that they regarded as appearances of the risen Jesus. He also describes this scholarly recognition as the single most crucial development in this field of study in recent years. See Habermas, Gary "Resurrection Research from 1975 to the Present: What Are Critical Scholars Saying?" (2005). *Faculty Publications and Presentations*. Paper 9. Also at http://digitalcommons.liberty.edu/sor_fac_pubs/9

64. The fact that many of the early Christians were tortured and killed for their beliefs is described not only in the New Testament and other early Christian writings, but also by Roman writers, such as Tacitus, Suetonius, Juvenal and Pliny the younger.

"I really don't long for tea and biscuits right now," added John. "Please keep going!"

CHAPTER 21

DIVIDED THEY FALL

SHERLOCK TOOK OFF HIS jacket, his face now even more concentrated. He pulled his hand through his hair and shook himself. Like an athlete preparing himself for the final round, thought John inwardly.

Outside the window, darkness slowly began to fall. The first weekday of Holy Week approached its end. The atmosphere in the worn and torn lecture room also began to feel more tense.

"Let me go and fetch a couple of candles, to create a cosier atmosphere while we continue," said Judith.

Sherlock weighed the piece of chalk in his hand, found it a bit too short and changed to another one. He juggled a bit with it, meanwhile proposing some guidelines for the coming discussion:

"Now, I hope we can agree to skip explanations that include aliens, druids with unknown drugs, or gods who at lightning speed replace the crucified man, and so on? I suggest that we keep to alternatives that at least *some* scholars with some credibility might accept."

"Sounds terrific!" smiled Alex and fingered his doctoral ring. The wedding ring was back where it belonged, noted John, and felt gratitude over the events of the last couple of weeks. Judith soon returned with some block candles, which she placed on the teacher's pulpit. The group moved forward, closer to the blackboard. The candles lit up the immediate surroundings, while darkness grew deeper outside.

"While we've been wrestling with these basic facts, we've also touched upon some of the more reasonable suggestions for what might have happened that Passover in Jerusalem," began Sherlock. "Some of them seem to have fallen apart already before we began our investigation. As far as I've understood it, the apparent death hypothesis was pretty popular for some time." He lifted the chalk, and wrote under the headline *Possible explanations* high up on the right half of the blackboard: Jesus never died on the cross.

"At least it was popular up until late 19th century," interjected Alex. "By now, we have better knowledge of crucifixions. It's also too bizarre to imagine that the devastated disciples would have been convinced if they had encountered a lethally wounded man who, against all odds, had managed to crawl out of his burial cloth, out of the tomb and all the way back to his followers. If that had been the case, they would soon have fetched medical aid in order to—if possible—save this horribly wounded man. One thing they definitely would *not* have done was to shout 'The Messiah has come, and death is defeated!' Therefore, this hypothesis is completely abandoned among scholars."

Sherlock grabbed the duster and erased what he'd just written.

"I assume that explanations like 'Everybody got lost on the way to the tomb' and such also fall, when we look at the facts here on the left-hand side," said John, thoughtfully.

"True, and as we've established that the tomb was actually empty on the Sunday morning, it's also there we need to put our main focus," continued Sherlock grimly.

"Let's take the alternatives one by one and see where we end up," suggested John.

Sherlock wrote: Enemies or outsiders stole the body. He turned round to his audience:

"So, what does the panel say about this plucky proposal?"

"Unthinkable!" cried Judith Barkley.

"Accepted. But why?" asked Sherlock.

"Well, it's just that . . . " she continued. " . . . why would the Romans, or the Jewish Sanhedrin steal the body of the man they'd just managed to execute?"

"Exactly so," smiled Sherlock confirmingly. "Finding the motive is a crucial point in every investigation. There simply wasn't any reason for Jesus' enemies to suddenly hide away his body, now that they'd finally succeeded in getting rid of the problem."

"There was also a clear motive in keeping the tomb intact," said Alex. "The enemies were very familiar with how earlier Messianic movements had fallen to pieces as soon as their leaders had passed away. Therefore, they would have had everything to lose by provoking the disorder that a lost body might create."

"And no ancient source suggests any unknown grave robber, nor does a possible motive exist," added Sherlock. "We may thus expunge also this hypothesis as unthinkable," stated the detective and went up and did just that.

"Then let's try the more popular alternative that the disciples took things in their own hands," suggested John.

Sherlock wrote again: The disciples stole the body.

"This seems to have been considered to be one of the strongest alternatives," admitted Sherlock. "We know, for instance, that this hypothesis was commonly accepted among Jews in the latter half of the first century."

"Still, I have the impression that you see substantial problems with it," commented Alex.

"I do. If you look to the left, you see point number six. How are we to interpret the body snatcher alternative in relation to this piece of fact?"

John read silently: "The disciples were fully convinced that their message of the resurrection was true." He felt how his head began to spin. Could it be the lack of oxygen in the room? he wondered, before Judith interrupted his thoughts.

"Isn't this point incredibly simple? Nobody dies for something they know to be false, and that's it."

"On the other hand, we've discussed before that people can die for weirder things than this," objected John, fully aware what answer he was going to receive. But he still felt the need to turn every possible stone.

"The main difference is obviously that the people you mention actually believe in the things they're prepared to give their lives for," countered Sherlock, just as John had guessed. "Those who flew airplanes into buildings in the September 11th attacks *believed* very strongly that they gave their lives for a good cause. We might say they were deluded, or that they had drawn bad conclusions, but nobody can say that they weren't devoted to their beliefs."

"We may also add that even if the disciples—against all expectation—first would have stolen the body, and thereafter had these very palpable experiences of a living Jesus, the case with James and Paul still remains to be explained," said Alex. "Neither of them would have been convinced merely by the message that the body was gone. On the contrary, they would most probably have been satisfied with the suggestion that Jesus' followers had somehow abducted his corpse."

Sherlock lifted his hand, ready to erase: "Thus, these are a few of the reasons why almost all scholars today have abandoned the hypothesis as unthinkable."

Without remorse, he let the duster remove also this alternative, and once more turned to his little audience. By now, it was completely dark outside. None of them had thought of turning on the fluorescent lamps on the ceiling and destroying the intimate feeling in the room.

"Now is the time when this case gets really tricky," said Sherlock resolutely. "Feel free to add other alternatives—but as far as I can see it, we only have two suggestions left to work with." The detective turned to the blackboard, hesitated for a second, but then wrote two words next to each other:

Hallucinations   Resurrection

None of the others said a word. "Well then, what do you say?" asked Sherlock impatiently. "Where do the strengths or weaknesses lie in these two alternatives?"

"I can encourage you by saying that these two are the alternatives that almost all current scholars choose between as well," clarified Alex. "Now, the second alternative is unthinkable in a closed universe. Still, it's quite feasible if we imagine at least a small possibility that God exists, and has the ability to intervene in the world. This is, by the way, also a possibility that the vast majority of mankind hold as true," he added.

"How should we view the first alternative then?" continued Sherlock. "I'm ready to continue trying this as far as necessary."

John took the opportunity to add some personal experiences. "I know from the theatre of war that both soldiers and civilians under severe stress may experience hallucinations of different kinds. However . . . "

Sherlock gave him a nod, encouraging him to go on.

"Well, the problem is that these kinds of optical illusions or hallucinations are always individual—not joint experiences, and they're usually very confused and surreal. As far as we've seen, though, the accounts from the disciples appear to be very sober when they begin to preach the resurrection. Their experiences are distinctly joint, and they also seem to have happened in different circumstances, which isn't normally the case with hallucinations. You remember when we repeated the testimonies together with Lestrade: sometimes they were individual, sometimes in group, sometimes outdoors, sometimes indoors, sometimes . . . "

"I know!" interrupted Sherlock. "I see this weakness."

Judith Barkley felt the urge to give input to the conversation: "Surely you can imagine a follower of Jesus having a mystical revelation in a vulnerable situation. But James and Paul—they were absolutely not the kind of people who would allow themselves to be overtaken by some kind of spiritual experience with no connection to reality. Their changed points of view need to be explained in another way."

Sherlock tapped a foot impatiently. He managed to avoid interrupting this time.

"Last but not least, we have another problem, which I consider to be completely insurmountable," added Alex. "That is the empty tomb. There could have been enormous numbers of people who claimed to have met a risen Jesus. That still wouldn't have helped. If there had been *any* human remains left in the tomb, it would have been the easiest thing in the world to bite the head off this new movement, just by displaying the decomposing . . .

"I *know!*" Sherlock could no longer hide his frustration. "Any rational person can see these problems. But we have to carry on, trying to find a way forward. We just have to!"

The great detective seemed to have had enough of the exposition, and he burst out of the room. Despite the dusky lighting, John noted that he had seldom seen his friend so dogged.

Out in the parking he soon found his vanished companion.

"I took the liberty of bringing your coat," said John softly. Sherlock took the garment, gave his flatmate an insecure smile, and put the coat on.

The journey home proceeded in silence.

CHAPTER 22

VISIONS AND REVELATIONS

TUESDAY CAME AND WENT. Sherlock was as hard to find as he usually was when he had no intention of keeping in touch. Wednesday afternoon, though, John received a text message.

<Need your help. Corner of Dorset Sq>

John started inwardly. Sherlock apparently hadn't lost his ability to act. Whatever he needed help with, it was still a positive sign that he got in contact and had something going.

The spring day was cloudy and windy. John quickly put on a spring jacket and made the short walk down to Dorset Square. At the corner there was already someone waiting. It was Inspector Lestrade from Scotland Yard.

"John!" he called with a relieved voice. "I'm glad that you've shown up too. Any idea if Sherlock has sobered up since last time?"

John smiled back. "Well, the case he's wrestling with seems to be a trickier one than usual. Was it you who called for him today?"

"No," replied the police inspector. "I got the message half an hour ago that Sherlock Holmes needed my assistance, and that I was to show up here." Lestrade began to look worried. "I'll admit that I hesitated before I dropped what I was doing, in order to come here. I mean, is he of sound mind right now?"

John didn't find the time to deliver the calming answer he wished to give, before Sherlock called them from the opposite street corner.

136

"Hi there! Excellent of you to show up on such a short notice. Could you come over here?"

He seemed to be back to his normal alert and inspired self, reflected John. They walked over the road to their friend.

"Any tough cases at the moment, Lestrade?" Sherlock greeted him with a good-natured smile.

"That would be you, I guess," he answered evasively. "I think I understand you less by the day, Sherlock. What are you up to this time? I don't have all day, you know."

"I wonder if you could accompany me down to this basement for a moment?" asked Sherlock, equally jolly as before. "There's a detail I'd like to run past you."

John and Lestrade strolled after him. Sherlock led them down some cellar stairs, which seemed to have had their glory days long ago. The door was unlocked, and with a bow the detective showed them inside.

"It's no Buckingham Palace, but I hope it'll do to show you something interesting."

The sound from the three men's steps echoed through the dark corridor, before Sherlock turned left, opened a thick door and stepped over the high concrete threshold, into a bare room with some sheets hanging from two clothes lines. A drying room, apparently, thought John. A bare light bulb spread a cold light, and a fan heater went at full speed. The temperature was disturbingly high.

"Do take a seat," said Sherlock, pointing at two old steel chairs in a corner, and then turned off the heating unit. The silence became palpable to the two bewildered men. They pulled out the simple chairs and cautiously sat down.

"There we are. Allow me to excuse myself for a moment. I'll be right back." Sherlock bowed again, turned on his heel and disappeared. The door closed with a bang, and the footsteps outside died away.

Those left inside had the same instinct, and quickly rid themselves of their jackets. Even in their shirtsleeves they soon began to feel sweaty. A minute passed by without a sound being heard.

"What in heaven's name do you think he's up to this time?" whispered Lestrade, peeking under a sheet to make eye contact.

John replied with a nervous laugh: "Well, that's not easy to guess, I can tell you. It's only been a couple of weeks since the last time I got dragged into another basement, where our detective friend was experimenting with . . . crucifying himself."

Lestrade was taken aback: "What if he tries to bury himself alive today?" he said with a restrained laugh. "Nothing surprises me any more when Sherlock Holmes is involv . . . "

At that second, the light went out. Both of them twitched. A strong sense of unease awoke in both of them. It took a moment before their pupils began to adapt to the faint light from the small cellar window up by the ceiling. The sheets hung there, just as heavy and still as before. Without a word, Lestrade moved his chair closer to John's. The scraping from the chair felt uncomfortably loud in the silence. Both men breathed heavily in the heat, and looked eagerly towards the door. Still, no steps were heard from outside. They sat there, alone in the stifling drying room, without knowing what to expect next.

But what was that? John quickly turned his head to check what he'd registered in the corner of his eye. Some big, shapeless thing seemed to have moved over there in the corner, behind the fan heater. He rose slowly, with a quickly increasing pulse. The shapeless thing in the corner gradually started to unfold itself. John opened his eyes wide in growing terror. The heap rose and turned into a snake, a giant snake, a monster.

"Watch out—the snake!" he hissed. "Run!" John threw himself on the door, but it was locked from the outside. In panic he turned round, searching for something to use as a weapon.

From Lestrade, there was no help to be found. He had kicked his chair over, and now gesticulated like a maniac in the opposite corner of the cellar room.

"Get away, damned creatures!" he screamed wildly and waved his arms frantically upwards, while somehow trying to cover his face under one of his arms.

Meanwhile, John could see how the snake rose to a man's height. In his vulnerable position, John acted involuntarily. He grabbed the heating unit, and with a strength that he otherwise would never have been capable of, he pulled it loose from its place and threw it with all his power at the beast.

At the same moment, the light came back on, and in through the door came Sherlock. Without a word, he took some quick steps up to the cellar window and opened it as much as he could. Both John and Lestrade sank down on the floor, shivering in shock. Lestrade couldn't stop his tears, once the tension began to dissipate. The men could no longer see another living being in the cellar room, apart from themselves.

Sherlock cautiously lifted one of the fallen chairs back up, and took a seat. The two others continued to lay on the floor with staring eyes and intermittent breaths.

"I'm terribly sorry that . . . you were so horror-stricken." Sherlock seemed to be fumble for words. "It was absolutely not my intention to induce such an intense effect."

John rolled over on his back, closed his eyes, and tried to come to terms with what he'd just experienced.

"What . . . was . . . that?" he finally stuttered.

"Let me first ask what you saw," replied Sherlock. "But do take the time you need," he hurried to add.

"Horrible—just horrible!" began Lestrade. He had to take a pause between the words, in order to catch his breath again. "From somewhere up in the ceiling came suddenly . . . a whole pack of bats. Huge, hideous bats. Eyes glowing, teeth gleaming. And how they screeched—my God!"

The hardened crime investigator propped himself up on one elbow, wiped a tear off his face and shook his head. "I've seen many horrid things over the years. But I can honestly say that I've probably never been as terrified as just now."

"Bats? said John, bewildered."Wh . . . ? Didn't you see the monstrous snake?" John looked over at the fan heater, which now lay smashed beneath the open window, bearing witness that something quite remarkable had happened just minutes ago.

Lestrade looked exhausted when he shook his head and said: "I fear that those bats will haunt my dreams for some time to come."

"Different experiences. Distinctly different experiences," mumbled Sherlock, with a somewhat vacant look on his face.

For the first time since Sherlock returned, Lestrade turned his head and looked furiously at the detective. His cheeks were glowing red with anger: "Perhaps you'd better tell us now what the hell this was all about?"

The edge in Lestrade's voice made Sherlock adopt a considerably softer tone than usual:

"I repeat . . . I definitely didn't mean to scare anyone this much." He got up and closed the window again. "I think we're OK now." Sherlock picked up the other chair, and pointed in a somewhat awkward manner. "Please take a seat. I can stand."

The two men on the floor pulled themselves together and managed to get seated.

"For some time I've kept a few ampoules of hallucinogen at home," began Sherlock.

John looked upset: "Where exactly, if I may ask?"

"I've got an odd Persian slipper. God knows where the other one's gone . . . This is where I store this type of stuff." Sherlock turned to Lestrade. "No, no, you don't have to issue a search warrant. This was the last contents of the slipper. I've now seen what effect the hallucinogen causes. I won't use it again. Well, at least not on law-abiding people . . . "

"But how did you release the gas into the room?" By now, Lestrade was beginning to get some strength back in his voice.

Sherlock pointed up at a corner between wall and ceiling, where a ventilator was visible.

"There. Easily accessible from the laundry room next door, where there's also a switch for the light bulb in here. By the way, you might have noticed a sign by the entrance, saying that all electric appliances down here will be replaced within the next couple of weeks," Sherlock added in an excusatory voice, nodding towards the wreckage of what had a couple of minutes ago been a fully functioning fan heater. "Now, come, let's get out of here. We've seen more than enough."

†

Outside in the fresh air, Sherlock showed his friends to a bench, then quickly rushed over the street, only to return a few minutes later with two large smoothies.

"Please accept these as some type of consolation, I hope they might at least partially redress the experience down there."

John managed a little smile on the inside. At the end of the day, it was somewhat refreshing to see this emphatic side, which Sherlock so seldom exposed. Without a word, the three men sat there for some minutes, side by side. Two of them guzzling through straws, the third one seemingly absent, staring in front of him, intensely thinking. Finally, Sherlock couldn't keep quiet any more:

"If I may return to what you experienced a moment ago, it was evident that you found it quite terrifying. Now, afterwards—would you say that what you experienced was actually real?"

"I think it's enough that you exposed us to danger for body and soul," replied Lestrade bitterly. "You don't have to add insult to injury, by treating us like imbeciles. It's perfectly evident that it didn't happen for real!"

"There were no snakes, no bats with glowing eyes," said John and circumspectly took the last swig of the smoothie. "Nothing of what we saw was real. You drugged us, we weren't in full possession of our senses."

"Now I want you to be absolutely honest with me," said Sherlock with emphasis. He stood up and turned towards the other men. "When you saw the snake and the bats, were you at that moment fully convinced that they were real?"

"You saw for yourself, didn't you," John replied without hesitation. "It was a truly gruesome experience. Do you think I would have thrown a fan heater into the wall, if I hadn't felt that my life was at stake?"

"Please bear with me, just one last question: Now, afterwards, you're equally convinced that this didn't happen in the physical world?"

John nodded, thoughtfully. The flashes coming from Lestrade's eyes said more than enough. Sherlock started to walk round among the pigeons, who eagerly waited for something to eat.

"This is crucial," he mumbled, his gaze lost someplace else. "This is absolutely crucial."

He looked up once more, and continued: "You realize that we've reached an exceedingly important step on the way to solving this riddle?"

"I think you'll have to move back a few stages if we're to follow you," said John.

"Don't you see? A person may have an incredibly strong and convincing experience, which might nevertheless lack all connection to the real world. It may be imagination, a psychosis, a hallucination—you name it. However, as soon as a person in this situation recovers, they always see the unreal character of the experience—totally independent of how real you earlier experienced the event. Are you with me?"[65]

---

65. Michael Licona has described these types of experiences among people who under heavy stress and exhaustion have had hallucinations. He did not do this by performing the kind of advanced experiment that Sherlock does here, though, but by interviewing American elite fighting forces about their experiences from a part of their training which is called "Hell week," where many of them had hallucinations. Here too, their experiences differed clearly from each other, and none of their visions included the other soldiers. They were very distinctly individual, but still appeared very real to them at the time. Nevertheless, all of those interviewed realized afterwards that their experiences had no connection to the real world. These interviews are referred to in Habermas/Licona *The Case for the Resurrection of Jesus*, p 106–107.

They both nodded and looked down at the ground. Sherlock continued with firmness:

"For those who claimed to have met the risen Jesus, there is no sign at all that any single one of the reported witnesses changed their minds, or even showed hesitation later on. Not just a few, but all the witnesses held to their experience for the rest of their lives. They did so in danger and under threat, all the way to a martyr's death. This is an incredibly important insight. I cannot overestimate its weight in this case."

Sherlock made a rhetorical pause, before he wrapped it all up: "Gentlemen, I once again extend my deepest apologies for the discomfort I caused you. It's time to move on."

His coat fluttered around him, as Sherlock turned and with swift steps hurried away towards the nearest tube station. Still sitting on the bench were two men, each with an empty mug in his hand, staring speechlessly at each other, both with a pair of eyebrows raised in sheer surprise.

CHAPTER 23

ALL SAID AND DONE

GOOD FRIDAY HAD COME. Even in the twenty-first century, the city pulse in London was remarkably slower, compared to other days of the year. In the sky, the clouds and the sun struggled with each other for supremacy. On a promenade down by the south shore of the Thames, two men were walking side by side.

"Have we reached the finish-line?" asked the slightly shorter one.

"I suspect that's the case," replied the taller one.

They stopped, and looked over to the other side of the river. In the silence of the day, they could hear the croaking from the ravens sitting on the walls of the Tower. Someplace from above, they suddenly heard other bird calls. The two men looked up, and could see a formation of swans passing over their heads, continuing across the Thames. The large number of white birds made the ravens take to flight, and flap down behind the secure walls. The bevy of swans descended, and chose to land on the river.

The two men resumed their walk.

"Is there really no other way out?" wondered the short one, just to make sure.

Sherlock Holmes once more made a halt, and looked at his companion.

"John, we've tried every possible and impossible explanation. Still, in the light of facts, they've collapsed, one by one. After having performed the experiment with the hallucinogenic gas . . . "

Sherlock made one more effort to excuse what happened down in the cellar: "I'm truly sorry for how the experience affected you. However, this experiment made it perfectly clear that no matter how strong an experience may be, a normal person still rejects it afterwards, if they find it probable that the experience lacked connection to reality. Now, if we are to put any trust at all in human narratives, we must also listen to honest testimonies that people stick to even in the face of death—especially if these testimonies also give the only credible explanation to all other circumstances. In this case there just isn't any other explanation that fits better with the facts we have."

John Watson listened patiently. He looked up to the sky, where the clouds at the moment seemed to have the upper hand in the battle over the vault of heaven.

"And this would apply even if the remaining explanation speaks against what we otherwise hold to be true?"

Sherlock once again looked out across the river.

"There have been several occasions in my business, where I've thought that all alternatives were closed, and that the case simply seemed insoluble. There are times where I've had to give up, I'll admit that. Sometimes, though, I've decided to carry on anyhow, in those cases where facts have continued to stare me in the face, saying that there *must* be another opening somewhere in the deadlock. Every time I've done so, this opening has always appeared, sooner or later."

John scratched with his foot against the ground.

"You mean that the explanation that you now seem to lean towards also is the only one that makes use of all the loose pieces of the jigsaw?"

The detective thought for a second, before he replied with a parallel:

"John, all popular movements have a beginning. No football team would have any supporters if the club was not founded. There never would have been a Beatlemania if there hadn't been a band from Liverpool who wrote songs and recorded albums."

Sherlock pointed over towards the other side of the Thames.

"From here we can see at least three church towers within very short distance. The Christian movement had a beginning, too. And we have a pretty good picture of when and where it was. This movement claims to be founded on a very distinct first event. Now, if this event never took place, the birth of the world's largest movement, with billions of adherents, becomes completely incomprehensible."[66]

John nodded.

"Have you spoken more with Alex?" he wondered cautiously.

Sherlock shook his head. "Not since Monday."

John did his best to bring some order to all the thoughts in his head, and tried to put the events of the past weeks in a more personal perspective: "You know, I'm confirmed, just like most other British people. But you know how it is—in these days you sort of push aside the religious questions to some kind of mystical sphere, where you don't think that much about what is actually true or not."

"A completely untenable life strategy, at least when it comes to those questions that can be studied rationally," mused Sherlock. "One thing that I've appreciated with this case is that we've been doing just that. Cross, nails, graves and linen shroud. Those are tangible objects, things that can be analysed by normal, scientific methods. And at the end of the day, I have to admit that all arrows point in the same direction."[67]

John remembered the rule that Sherlock so often used to remind him of: "I think your regular point goes something like this: You should pursue an investigation until all unthinkable or practically impossible explanations have fallen away, and only one remains. The alternative that remains standing, no matter how far-fetched it may seem, no matter whether you like it or not, this alternative still has to be . . . "

"The truth."

They both stood silent. John picked up the conversation once more:

66. William Lane Craig, world renowned resurrection scholar, summarizes the matter: "There simply is no plausible natural explanation available today to account for how Jesus' tomb became empty. If we deny the resurrection of Jesus, we are left with an inexplicable mystery." Craig, William Lane *Reasonable Faith*, p 377

New Testament historian NT Wright puts it like this: "[T]he historian may and must say that all other explanations for why Christianity arose, and why it took the shape it did, are far less convincing *as historical explanations* than the one the early Christians themselves offer: that Jesus really did rise from the dead on Easter morning, leaving an empty tomb behind him." Wright, NT "Jesus' Resurrection and Christian Origins" *Gregorianum*, 2002, 83/4.

67. Sir Lionel Luckhoo, in Guinness' Book of World Records declared to be the world's most successful lawyer, summarizes the evidence in the following way: "I say unequivocally that the evidence for the resurrection of Jesus Christ is so overwhelming that it compels acceptance by proof which leaves absolutely no room for doubt." Luckhoo, Lionel *The Question Answered: Did Jesus Rise from the Dead?* quoted in Strobel, Lee *The case for Christ* (Zondervan 1998) p 389

"Well, if that's the case, what relevance would this have to us here and now?"

Sherlock pushed down his hands deep into his coat pockets.

"I don't know, John . . . Right now it feels as though I don't know anything at all."

Once more they looked out across the river. On the other side, the swans seemed to be finished with their short break. They flew up into the air, and continued on their route. Sherlock gave a deep sigh, turned to John and said:

"I need some time to think. See you."

With quick strides, he took the way up through the park behind them, and was gone.

CHAPTER 24

DAWN BREAKS

JOHN TURNED HIS CAR into the small forest road, stopped, and turned off the engine. He looked at his watch. Three in the morning. None the less, he was wide awake. He hadn't seen a trace of Sherlock Holmes since he disappeared Friday afternoon. The thoughts had spun around in John's head during the whole Easter Eve, though when he'd gone to bed at his regular time in the evening, he'd soon fallen asleep. Around one o' clock in the morning, he'd awoken with a gnawing unease in the pit of his stomach. What had happened to his companion? He couldn't have injured himself in any way, could he? John had got up and peeked in through Sherlock's open bedroom door, and realized that he still hadn't come home.

The anxiety became so strong that it forced John to get dressed, leave the building and get into the car in order to—if possible—find his friend somewhere in the Easter night. While driving, he tried to think logically. Where could Sherlock have gone? John decided to try the way out to the forest outside Hertford, where Alex had said that the Easter Mass was going to take place.

Normally, when Sherlock had solved a case, an atmosphere of calmness and intellectual satisfaction would settle over him. This was no regular case, though. This time, John felt ill at ease when he thought back to the frustration Sherlock had shown when he'd rushed away from the south bank of the Thames.

He got out of the car and shut the door. Despite his carefulness, the slam sounded loud in the silence of the night. The mid-April weather had brought warmer winds from south. The spring night was starlit, but still relatively mild. John walked hastily along the path towards the glade where the service was scheduled to be. After a bend, he suddenly spotted the outline of a man in front of him. It wasn't Sherlock—that much was sure. At the sound of John's steps, the man turned round. John immediately realized that it was another familiar person.

"John?" said Alex Barkley in a hesitating voice, and held up his hands over his eyes, to see more clearly in the moonlight that shone through the trees. John went up to him.

"You here?" asked John, in honest surprise. His voice automatically became slightly more quiet than normal in the darkness of the night.

"I sort of had an . . . impulse to come here beforehand tonight."

John nodded slowly.

"Me too. Have you seen him during the last . . . " John glanced at the luminous hands on his watch " . . . the last forty hours or so?"

Alex shook his head. "I was coming here anyway. Shall we continue down to the glade?"

The two men walked the short distance that remained. The forest was still silent, no birds showed any signs of waking up yet. Just where the forest plateau went over in a little slope down to the glade, they both stopped.

Down on the slope they saw a familiar silhouette of a man, dressed in an equally familiar coat. His back was turned towards the two night wanderers, his face towards the moon.

"Shall we go to him together?" whispered Alex.

"Not necessary," whispered John back. "Now I know he's in safe hands. I'll be back in time for the service at dawn."

He gave the priest a friendly pat, turned round and began his retreat. Such an inconceivably strange coincidence, he thought on the way back. When he'd got back to the car, he once again looked at his watch. Four o' clock, and still pitch dark. He sat down in the driver's seat. Why not rest a little while and do at bit of thinking before it was time to go down to the glade again.

Two minutes later, John Watson was in deep sleep.

†

On the slope under the stars, two men sat together in silence, their eyes fixed upon the full moon, which still shone from a cloudless night sky. After a while Sherlock began to speak:

"One of the most important qualities of a friend is the ability to share silence together. I appreciate that."

"How are you feeling right now?" asked Alex gently.

Sherlock took some time before answering. The two men's breaths were heard clearly in the quiet of the night. Alex thought for a moment that he could also hear the detective's heartbeat, though maybe it was just his imagination.

"I'm . . . confused. I'm getting nowhere. I've been walking, thinking, but I can't find any peace. Sleeping is out of the question. Normally, when I've solved a case, I can with a clear conscience let it go, and then move on to other tasks. But I sense that this case is . . . different."

"That makes two of us," said Alex confirmingly. "You've been of invaluable use to me and my wife. The last couple of weeks have been different from any lent period I've ever experienced."

Sherlock gave a short laugh: "Yes. We can agree on that."

Alex waited for some seconds before he continued: "Allow me to think aloud for a little while: might it be that your normal cases never involve you personally? When you've solved them, you can readily delegate the rest to the people you've assisted. However, this time, you perhaps have an inkling that the solution to this case might concern all people in all historical eras, and you're not really sure how to handle this on a personal level. Do you think this might be an adequate description of your current reaction?"

Sherlock gave the thought a moment to land.

"Yes—maybe." For the first time he turned to Alex, and looked into his moonlit face. "I get very uncomfortable when I don't feel that I'm in control. If the solution to this case lies where all the facts indicate, would it have any practical implications for a modern person's life and purpose? I don't know if I'm ready for anything like that."

Alex smiled.

"You know, I don't think that anyone, ever, anywhere owns full control of his or her life. I fear that this is a sad myth that the modern man has built over himself. I only know one thing: the resurrection of Jesus from the dead has given my life a whole new light. It gives hope, peace and meaning to me personally. But also to millions of other people around the globe."

He made a pause: "Still, none but the individual can decide how he or she ought to deal with the great event that we'll soon gather to celebrate."

In the east, one could see the first slight tint of orange in the sky.

"The time is almost here, my friend." Alex patted Sherlock on the shoulder. "I have to go get Judith and fetch the rest of the things we need for mass."

The priest went, and left Sherlock there to himself.

†

An hour later, the light of dawn had broken through the trees. The congregation were seated on blankets in the glade. Up on the slope, under an oak, sat the detective. His body was tired, but his mind fully concentrated.

At the front of the gathering, Alex Barkley stood up, now dressed in his finest chasuble. He turned to those assembled, lifted his hands and called in a loud voice:

"Christ is risen!"

As one man, the congregation rose and gave their response:

"Truly, He is risen!"

The priest repeated the same phrase, this time even louder:

"Christ is risen!"

This time, Sherlock Holmes too stood up, on trembling legs. In a whispering voice, the response came also from his lips:

"Truly, He is risen."

CPSIA information can be obtained
at www.ICGtesting.com
Printed in the USA
LVHW101305150519
617936LV00018B/455/P